A Future, Forged

(A **Kalima Chronicles Prequel**)

By Aiki Flinthart

2020

p2

Thank you to the readers who have enjoyed my other books enough to leave nice reviews and to let me know. Because of you, I keep writing.

And...as always...thanks to my husband for his patience and encouragement. Seriously. Patient. Unbelievably patient.

A Cataloging-in-Publications entry for this title is available from the National Library of Australia.

ISBN-13: 978-0-9945928-8-0 (Trade Paperback)
ISBN-13: 978-0-9945928-7-3 (e-book)
CAT Press
PO Box 3388, Darra
QLD 4076, Australia

Discover other titles by Aiki Flinthart
at: **www.aikiflinthart.com**
Including:

The Blackbirds Novels (Historical Fantasy)
Blackbirds Sing (#1)

The Ruadhan Sidhe Novels (YA Urban Fantasy)
Shadows Wake (#1)
Shadows Bane (#2)
Shadows Fate (#3)

The Kalima Chronicles (YA Adventure/Fantasy)
IRON (#1)
FIRE (#2)
STEEL (#3)

The 80AD series (YA Adventure/Fantasy)
80AD Book 1: *The Jewel of Asgard*
80AD Book 2: *The Hammer of Thor*
80AD Book 3: *The Tekhen of Anuket*
80AD Book 4: *The Sudarshana*

Maps of Kalima

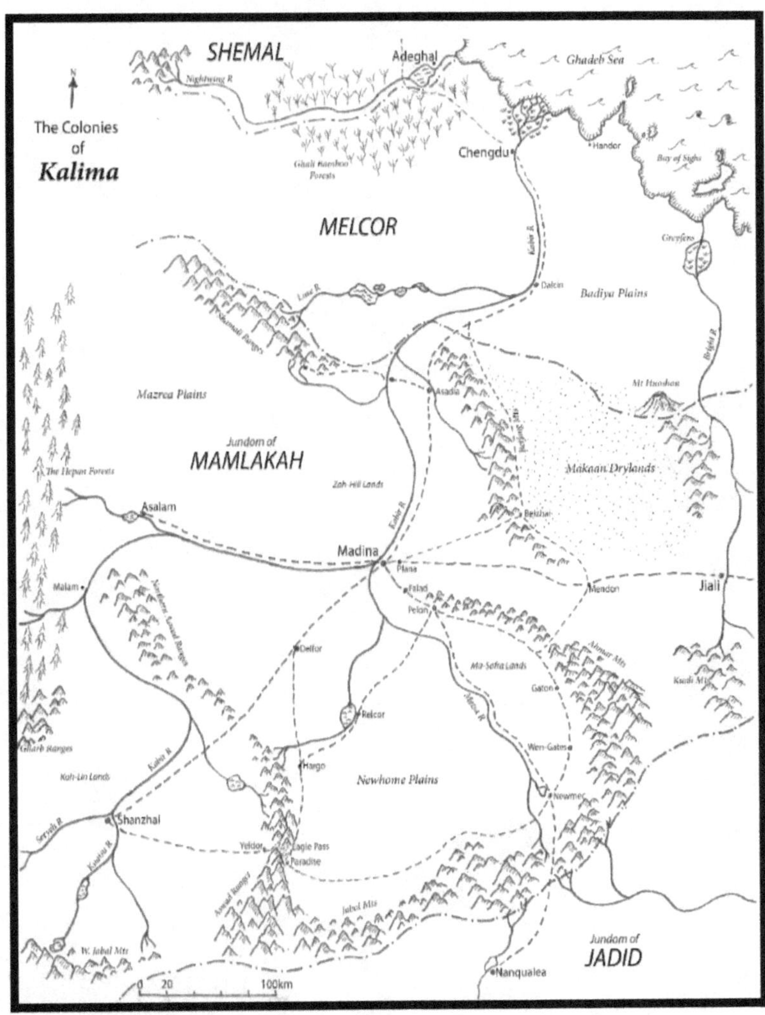

City of
Asalam
Key
1. Chinshi
2. Qin-Turner Residence
3. Grey-Saud Residence
4. East Gate prison
5. Weishi House
6. Jiaoji House
7. Healer House
8. Artist House
9. Miner House
10. Merchant House
11. Trades House
12. Messenger House
Dahab Hot Springs
Dahab Falls
Migong Slums
Dahab River
To Madina
N
2
7
3
5
6
12
1
11
10
4
9
8
0 50 100m

A Future, Forged

Aiki Flinthart 2020

NOTE:
This book is written with AUSTRALIAN
SPELLING/ENGLISH,
not USA spelling/English.
Don't panic.

This is prequel to IRON, first in the *Kalima Chronicles.*
A Future, Forged is set 200 years before IRON

CHAPTER ONE

Only the past can free the future

TEYA

Teya looked back twice as she ran. They were still coming. Gouri! Why wouldn't they leave her alone? She scowled and dodged south.

She ducked sideways to avoid a cart, and jagged around the corner of a bakery before the city guardsmen spotted her change of direction. A stack of old riceflour sacks offered refuge. She collapsed behind them, against the warm sulcrete-and-stone wall, panting. Overhead, slivers of pale green sky showed between the neatly-tiled rooflines. The burnt-orange sunlight created purple patches of shadow dark enough to hide a thief good at being invisible.

Perrin slid in beside her, his thin body shaking but an indomitable grin on his dirt-smudged face. His shortened, maimed left leg didn't slow him much anymore. He tucked a hand into hers and she squeezed it. His quick breaths puffed little clouds into the sharp, late-autumn air.

Heavy footsteps clattered close to their hiding place. Two city junren-guards. They peered into the alley. Teya crouched lower and dragged Perrin's tousled blond head out of sight. She stared at the junren, through a gap in the sacks. Matching expressions of intent listening passed over their faces. They retreated into the broader street and ran off.

The sound of their boots on the cobbles faded and Perrin slumped against the wall with a thick-blown sigh. He lifted his bare left foot and massaged the swollen ankle.

'Twisted the stupid thing. Again.' Tears glistened but he pawed them away and grinned at Teya. 'Thought those junren were gonna catch us! What'd you get?'

Teya hefted a silver and turquoise brooch, turning it so the metal and green-blue stones gleamed in the afternoon light. Pickings in the rich northern areas of Asalam city were better, but the city guards were more alert, too. She'd been careless. It wouldn't happen again. Perrin needed her.

'I did it, didn't I? Was I good?' Perrin's gaze was fixed on her, eager. 'I watched you real close and I fell over when you winked at me, like we planned. But you might have to wink bigger next time. It was kinda hard to see.'

'I will, I promise. You're a pretty good little actor.' She managed a smile. 'And these rich people like to feel so goody-goody when they stop to help a poor little crippled boy who's hurt his leg.' She snorted. 'Like they care. They've forgotten you two seconds later.'

Perrin giggled. 'Maybe 'cause you've stolen their purse and they're a bit cranky.'

p16

She shrugged. 'Serves them right. Gouri jun-lovers all of them.' She quashed a familiar surge of anger and ruffled her brother's wild blond hair. 'They've got more'n they need, anyway.'

'How much will we get?' he whispered.

'Not sure. We'll have to go to Bretta's pawn shop, through the Migong slums, to sell it. She gives the best prices. But it's risky so late in the afternoon. Gangs'll be out patrolling.'

Perrin's smile widened. 'Worth it, though. We can eat for a week off that. You're the *best.*' He beamed and rested his head on her shoulder, wrapping his thin arms as far around her as they would go. Then his excitement vanished and he leaned back, his eyes dark. 'But the lady you stole it off. What if she has children to feed, too? Will she need it?'

Teya took in her six-year-old brother's distress and knew a twinge of guilt. What would their mother say if she knew Teya used her gift for thievery and dragged Perrin into it as well? Teya fingered her mother's little gold locket that hung on a strip of leather beneath her tunic. Inside was a delicate painting of Teya aged nine—six years before.

She clenched her teeth against the raw taste of bitterness. Nothing. Her mother would say nothing, for her chance to care about her children had been ripped away five years ago. She would understand that Teya did what it took to survive and protect Perrin.

'No,' she said. 'That woman was rich enough to feed fifty kids. They all are on this side of town. Sucking up to the juns. Especially now the Jun First is coming to town.'

A Future, Forged p17

'I s'pose.' He sighed. 'It would be nice to have a mother. Tell me again about her?'

'Later,' Teya said, shoving aside a familiar pang of longing and regret. 'We need to get home. Besides…' she hugged him to her side '…we don't need anyone else. We can trust each other. Look out for each other. Always.'

He nodded, sparkling with determination.

'Good,' she said. No-one else would help them, that was for sure. She didn't say that out loud, though. Perrin still had faith in people. How, after growing up in the Migong slums, she had no idea. But she couldn't bear to disillusion him. He'd learn.

She rose, reversed her Trades-House-brown jacket to display the Merchant-green side and twitched the hood up, hiding her distinctive auburn hair. She brushed a lock aside. The fine stuff wasn't quite long enough to tie into a man's mawei—and at fifteen she didn't look old enough to wear one.

But she was *not* wearing a woman's veil, so she was left pretending to be a boy until she couldn't hide any longer. If that meant forever, then so be it. Being a woman in the jundom of Mamlakah was nothing special, anyway. Good for nothing but having children.

The brooch she stuffed into a deep pocket, where it nestled with a silk purse holding measly two yinbi coins, and a fine gold necklace tugged from around the neck of a skinny old noblewoman with more money than sense.

Not a great haul, but one that would feed Perrin for a few days. Perhaps even get him a pair of shoes to fit his twisted foot.

She peered around the riceflour sacks and relaxed. No junren-guards.

The only people in sight were a group of workers clearing out a blockage in Asalam city's hotsprings water conduits. A man and two teenage boys in Trades House brown were gathered beside an open access hole. The boys worked a hand-pump of some sort, and fed a pipe and a length of rope into the depths. Steam and water splashed from hole.

A smaller boy, about Perrin's age, poked his wet head out. He removed a mask and the breathing pipe and said something to the man. Then he collected a hammer and chisel, put the mask and pipe over his face, and disappeared.

Teya shuddered. What a horrible job. Every day held the possibility of getting trapped in flooded pipes. Drowning.

Perrin's hand snuck into hers again. She kissed his forehead. Maybe thieving wasn't the worst thing he could be doing, after all.

She peeked around the corner again. Time to go. The sky was darkening to teal as the afternoon wore on. Clouds gathered in the west, obscuring the dull orange autumn-sun where it balanced on the roofs across the road. With night would come a curfew and they had a long walk to get to their hidey-hole shelter in the Migongs.

'C'mon,' she said. 'If we're quick we can get to Bretta's and home before first curfew bells.' Teya sauntered into the street and headed south, toward the river. Perrin half-skipped alongside, chattering even as Teya watched for more junren.

The houses deteriorated as they left the better parts of town, changing from stately sulcrete and bloodsandstone, glass-windowed mansions to rough-cut stone and bamboo slums with shuttered holes for windows and broken tiles or bamboo ply for roofs.

Bath houses changed from huge, stone constructions, surrounded by restaurants and shops, to timber shanties that leaked steam and attracted thieves and unveiled jiaoji-whores plying their trades.

Teya grimaced. How she longed for a good, hot bath. But she couldn't afford the better ones—where she could bathe in privacy—and the cheaper ones were notorious for forcibly taking young girls and lads into the whorehouses that lined the riverbank. Or for vanishing them altogether.

There had been a lot of that, lately. They never returned.

A winding road opened into a misshapen square where a half-dozen merchants, wearing dirtied-green, manned stalls holding inferior wares. A far cry from the silk-edged, gilded trinkets available in the markets close to the Jun First's huge home in the city centre.

Did the Jun First, Jenna Zah-Hill know that the people of Asalam called her extravagant, overdecorated country house "Chinshi"— "stupid thing"?

Teya sniffed at the thought. The Jun First was just a few years older than she was and had only visited Asalam twice that Teya could remember. Stayed safe and pampered in the capital, Madina. The jun probably didn't even know where Asalam was on a map.

Juns were all self-interested shazis.

She strode through the square, checking to make sure Perrin was still close.

Four women, all wearing much-patched robes of faded-floral bamboo-cloth, huddled around the steaming well, heads together. They turned as Teya and Perrin approached. Their eyes might be obscured by the traditional half-veil, but their scrutiny made Teya's shoulders twitch. She faded herself and Perrin from their view. The women fell to whispering.

As she passed a fruit stall, Teya filched two jilla fruit and hid herself from the stall-holder's notice. She ate one fruit in five large bites, and slurped at the tart scarlet juice, licking her fingers to catch each drop. The other fruit went to Perrin and he devoured it with messy speed, falling behind as he concentrated.

She rounded a corner and ploughed into a much larger body. A man. She stumbled and clutched at his belt. Habit brought her dagger hand up. Leather parted beneath the sharp bronze blade.

'I do apologise, young man,' a cultured voice said above her. An elegant, brown hand came to rest on Teya's shoulder. He smelled cleanly of soap and faintly of mel-oil.

Teya whipped her arms behind her and put on an innocent look. Too late to hide. 'Never mind, shenshi. My fault. Wasn't watching.' She managed a jerky half-bow and retreated, blending her image with the wall. He'd forget her in a moment.

She peeked sideways, pleased that Perrin had the sense to stay hidden.

The man dropped his hand to his hip in a habitual gesture. His night-black eyes widened. He glanced down. Then he tilted his head and stared straight at her.

Teya gaped. How could he see her?

CHAPTER TWO

TEYA

'Shenshi Dallan?' A black-clad weishi-bodyguard stepped forward. 'What is it?' Two more joined him, one a woman.

Teya swallowed, her heart thudding.

The dark-haired man gestured them away. 'I'll deal with him.'

The weishi exchanged confused looks. 'Who—?'

Dallan cut them off with a wave, focussed on Teya.

She clung tight to the objects in her hands and tensed. She'd backed herself against the wall, instead of into the alley. Nowhere to run. Jiche! Stupid mistake! Why could he see her? She couldn't even warn Perrin lest it give his position away.

But the man called Dallan surprised her. Rather than crying thief or setting his weishi on her, his sharp features softened into wryness. He flicked his cobalt-and-green tartan cloak over one shoulder and held out a palm.

'Return it and we'll say nothing of this, boy.' His dark eyes held a hint of hardness at odds with the gentle smile. His three weishi laid hands on their ceramic swords, their gazes passing, unseeing, over her position.

She produced the belt, her cheeks and stomach burning. In the last five years she'd been providing for Perrin, she'd never once been caught. No one saw her if she didn't want them to. Would he really do nothing, or would he turn her over to the junren now he had his things? That would be typical.

Dallan held the sliced-through strip of leather and fingered the ornate dagger-sheath. He sent Teya an ironic look.

With a sigh, she pulled the dagger from its place in the small of her spine. The blade glinted silvery in the orange sunlight.

'Steel!' she whispered. Light danced across the steel blade and played weakly in the milk-white stone set into the pommel. A knife like this was worth more than…well more than she could even imagine in coin.

'Yes,' Dallan replied. 'Earth steel, in fact. Over six hundred years old. Been in my family for twenty generations.' He plucked the blade from Teya and weighed it in his palm. 'My ancestor brought it with him to Kalima in the first colony ship, five hundred years ago.'

Teya sucked a quick breath. 'You're a first-family?' There had been five hundred families on that original ship. Twenty-one of them were the funding-families that later became the ruling juns. She let a spike of anger pass.

'Indeed,' Dallan said, inclining his head. His dark hair, held by a silver band into a fashionably-long mawei, slipped over his shoulder and lay against the grey silk of his jacket. Everything about him screamed wealth, from the sturdy leather of his boots to the spice-otter fur trimming his cloak.

p24

'You're not a jun?' she asked, feeling for the hilt of her bronze blade. First-families weren't so bad. Most were ordinary folk these days. The only difference was that they kept a family name instead of a kin-father name to show their parentage. But juns… she barely resisted the urge to spit at his feet.

His brows lifted. 'No. Why do you ask?'

'Nevermind.' Teya checked her surrounds. Could she run? Would he chase her down now he had his dagger back?

She wasn't far from the docks, which were a maze of warehouses and alleys. The stink of damp wood and rotting fish overwhelmed the Migong's usual stench of shit and garbage.

Close by, the Dahab River's warm, fast waters sloshed against timber pylons driven into the rocky river bottom. The vast Dahab Falls rumbled upriver to the west, hazing the air permanently with damp mist and washing the sun to faded orange.

But, even closer, shadows moved in the dark nooks between skewed buildings.

'Shenshi,' she muttered, eyeing two men whose ragged clothing hid wiry bodies made strong by desperation. 'You shouldn't be here. Get back to the north side of town, where you belong.'

Dallan swept a shrewd look at the ragtag crowd sidling closer from all directions. He nodded to his weishi, who drew weapons and faced outward, protecting their shenshi.

Teya shrank away but there was nowhere to go. Migong gangs, drawn by the smell of money, blocked every exit. If only Perrin had the sense to hide. Her mouth dried at the thought of him, small and alone, just around the corner. So close!

A large, bald man in a leather jacket shouldered to the fore of the crowd. He carried a weapon Teya had never seen before: a sickle-shaped bronze blade with a long chain attached to the handle, and a spiked bronze ball on the other end. He swung the ball and jerked his chin at Dallan.

'Give over the dagger, the sword and your purse and we might let you go.'

Dallan snorted. 'I find that unlikely.' He gestured at the gathering crowd. 'If you let us go, we'll be obliged to report to the city junren. And while you're welcome to almost anything I have, I can't give you the one thing you most want—my weapons. So we're left with two options.'

His smile thinned and his long fingers whitened on the hilt of his sword, on his left hip. 'You attack us and see how many survive. Four trained fighters against…' he did a swift count. 'Fifteen? I like our odds. Or you can leave with my purse and keep your arms and legs. Up to you,' he finished cheerfully.

'Zhal?' A wiry woman in maroon looked at the bald man.

He glared. 'C'mon. We can take them. I want that dagger and steel sword!' He released the spiked ball and it shot at Dallan's weishi. The crowd surged forward, blood-fever gleaming in their wild eyes.

Dallan and his weishi engaged, ceramic and steel ringing against bronze and wood. Teya pressed herself against the wall. She tried to slide sideways to the alley's safety; toward Perrin. Too much attention pinned her in place.

Her blood pounded, scattering her thoughts and making it impossible to shift notice away from herself. A toothless face leered in hers, blackweed-fouled breath gusting.

'You're *mine*, pretty one!' A thick-knuckled hand wrapped around Teya's wrist and dragged her away from Dallan and his weishi.

She jammed her dagger into the man's filthy arm and kicked at his shin. 'Get away from me!'

He swore and wrenched the dagger from her. The bloodstained blade slashed at her head. Teya threw herself sideways and the tip scored her shoulder. She slammed against the stone wall, gasping at the pain. Her assailant stalked closer, grinning in manic madness, turning the bronze dagger in bloodied fingers. From the back of his belt he produced another weapon—a vicious thing with four short, curved blades on the end of a short handle.

'Slavers from Melcor'll pay nice for a pretty-boy like you. Just have to tame you a bit, won't I?'

Teya shuffled along the wall, hoping to escape around the corner.

'No you don't, boy,' he growled. 'Hold still. I don't want to mess you up too much.'

She kept moving. Only a few more steps.

He threw the weapon. It flipped in the air. She tried to dodge. Misjudged. The longest blade drove into her shoulder. The same one he'd already tagged. But this time it dug deep into muscle and bone. Agonising. Blinding. Paralysing.

'Gaisi!' Dallan's voice growled nearby. A silvery blur passed over Teya's head. Her attacker collapsed; a heap of bloodsoaked rags with a steel sword buried in his gullet.

A strange warmth spread down the right side of her body. She gazed vaguely at Dallan, bemused as he swayed and spun before her.

'Shenshi!' one of Dallan's weishi cried. 'City junren. Coming this way. Quickly.'

'Catch him!' Dallan pointed at Teya. 'Bring him. We can't be found here.'

Her knees gave way and she sagged into waiting arms.

'Teya!' Perrin's cry was the distant wail of an orphaned lu-deer kid.

CHAPTER THREE

TEYA

Teya awoke to a warmth and softness she'd not experienced in five years. She snuggled deeper into thick sheets. A heavy quilt weighted her with lazy security and smelled of lavender and red-yin, Mother's favourite sleeping herb.

'Mother?' She swept a palm across the smooth linen. Pain stabbed through her shoulder and she snapped awake. Old, dark grief surged forth from its prison and threatened to overwhelm her. She pushed it aside automatically.

Overhead hung heavy drapes of midnight grey material, edged with copper thread. A window let faint, purplish light in around the edges of more thick curtains. The room was dark save for a single, flickering mel-oil lantern set next to the bed. A bed so huge Teya couldn't touch both sides.

She shot upright and flung the covers aside, holding her right arm against her stomach. The room tipped and spun. She swallowed hard against nausea and slid off the high mattress. A nearby chair provided a steadying brace. Her bare feet touched cold wood and she flinched.

She plucked at her clothing in dismay. In place of her grey bamboo-cloth shirt and trous, she wore an oversized man's shirt, the sleeves rolled up and the hem hanging to her knees. Underneath she was naked. Her own clothes were nowhere to be seen.

She clutched at her throat, her stomach knotting. Then she sighed. Her mother's locket was still there, around her neck. But where was everything else? And where was this house?

She tiptoed over to the massive window and twitched the heavy curtain aside. The room was on the ground floor, facing a wide, quiet street lined with tall, stately houses. Somewhere in the better parts of Asalam, then.

One of the two moons was out. Luna Yi's ruddy glow soaked the red-tiled roofs in pale blood and deepened the shadows to purple. Here and there, movement suggested people ignored the curfew, and the lack of city guards showed they went unpunished. Teya suppressed bitter understanding.

She raised her eyes to the Chinshi's two sandstone towers, blood-dark in the moonlight. The Jun First's country home, surrounded by a high, sandstone wall, dominated the city's skyline. If she could see the Chinshi's front she must be somewhere in Asalam's northwest quadrant. In the house of someone very well-off, judging by the rich furnishing.

But whose? And where was Perrin?

She returned to the bed and yanked out a drawer in the zitan-wood bedside table. Her things must be here somewhere.

The bedroom door clicked open and she snatched up the nearest possible weapon—a half-full glass of water—only to drop it when her fingers refused to work. The tumbler smashed on the timber floor, spraying her feet with cold water and sending shining slivers of glass sliding through the puddle.

'Don't move!' Dallan's voice whipcracked through the darkness.

Teya froze. His booted feet crunched and splashed through the water. He lifted her onto the bed. Then he calmly set the largest chunks of blue glass on a table, collected a towel from a pile of linen stacked on the chair and threw it across the mess on the floor. Finally, he drew up an elegant, spindle-legged chair and sat. Teya smoothed the shirt over her knees and wiped her wet feet on the bedlinen. She crossed her arms, holding her right elbow as her shoulder twinged.

Dallan pointed at her injury. 'Feeling alright?'

She nodded, considering him warily. 'Where am I? Where're my things?'

'You're welcome,' he said, a corner of his mouth lifting. 'You're in the house of a friend of mine. Your clothes are being washed and mended. Oh.' He rummaged in a pocket of his dark grey trous and dumped a small pile of items onto the bed. 'Here's the rest. Forgive me if I don't return the dagger quite yet.'

Teya thrust the tangle of jewellery into the silk purse and clutched it close with her left hand.

'Thank you. I have to go. I want my clothes.'

He cocked his head. 'My healer's of the opinion you should rest for a day. You lost a lot of blood. You were unconscious for two hours.'

'Two hours! Perrin! I have to…' She slid off the bed and ran to the door then paused. 'I can't go out like this.' She fisted the shirt.

Dallan moved toward her but stopped when she shrank away. 'I'm not going to hurt you, girl. Let me help. Who's this Perrin? Someone we can tell of your injury? Your father?'

'I'm wasting time. Get my clothes!'

'Child…' He paused. 'I can't keep calling you "girl" and "child". What's your name?'

'Teya,' she muttered. 'But it doesn't matter. Please. I have to go find him.'

'I'll take you home, myself, Teya. But will you answer me one question?'

She waited. Anything to get to Perrin. He would be worried. He always thought he could help by copying her ways, but he hadn't her skill at hiding in plain sight. If he took to thieving, thinking she wasn't coming home, he'd be caught for sure.

'Why couldn't my weishi see you, when we met in the street?'

Teya retreated until her shoulders pressed against the dark timber door. She wrenched at the handle and dashed out, running blindly along a shadowed hallway with no idea of how to escape.

But she must.

CHAPTER FOUR

TEYA

An arm caught her around the waist, knocking the wind from her lungs. She coughed and groaned as pain in her shoulder blurred her vision.

'Why the hurry, little one?' A woman wearing severe indigo robes with delicate embroidered copper and grey flowers twining up the sleeves held Teya's body against her own. Teya squirmed but could neither let go the precious purse nor use her injured right arm.

'Dal?' The woman glanced along the hall. 'Did you lose something?'

'She's quick, I'll give her that,' Dallan said. 'Shunu Nerina Qin-Turner, meet Teya who seems reluctant to give her family name.'

'Qin-Turner!' Teya stared at the elegant older woman. 'You're a jun!'

Nerina inclined her head. She rolled the indigo silk veil up onto her forehead, revealing rain grey eyes, wrinkled with amusement and deep-set in a narrow face.

'A Jun Fourth, in fact. Here in town by order of our illustrious Jun First, Jenna Zah-Hill, who is deigning to join us.' Her voice dripped with irony Teya didn't understand.

She released Teya, who put distance between them, raked the woman with scorn, and spat at her feet. The jun's lips pursed.

'Neri.' Dallan's low warning stopped whatever the woman might have said. 'She's a kid. She's afraid and you're scaring her.'

'I am *not* a kid. And I'm not scared. I'm *angry*. Let me go. I have to find my brother before he gets hurt. He was with me. He's only six.'

'There was no child…no, wait.' Dallan gazed off into middle distance, stroking his chin. 'A boy.' He held a palm out at hip height. 'About this tall? Blond hair and no shoes— something amiss with one foot?'

Teya nodded.

'Ah.' Dallan's expression became grave. 'I'm sorry. He was captured by the city junren, along with some of the people who attacked us. The junren must have thought him part of their group. They'll have taken him to the eastern gatehouse prison.'

The corridor seemed to sway again. Teya leaned against the bamboo-lined wall. Blood roared in her ears and echoed her mother's despairing cry as the cart carried her away.

'She said…' Teya sniffed and waited until she could control herself. 'The last thing my mother said was that I had

to look after him. He's my responsibility. What have I done?'
She turned to Dallan in desperation.

He held her arms and she flinched as pain stabbed into her
shoulder. His dark eyes searched hers.

'There was nothing you could have done. He'll be alright.'

'Dallan,' Neri murmured. 'Jun Fourth Gray-Saud has
taken charge of the city guards. He's announced capital
punishment for all crimes as a deterrent—'

He cast Neri a level look and she snapped her teeth shut.

'Grey-Saud! He's here?' Teya covered her mouth.
'Capital…you mean death? They'll kill Perrin?' She tugged
against Dallan's hold but he pinned her against the wall. 'Let
me go! I must save him.' She fought, struggling until
something ripped at the skin of her shoulder and blood stained
the pale shirt.

'Stop!' Dallan wrapped her in a tight embrace that
shocked her into obedience. 'Stop.' His tone gentled and he
held her away, his expression soft with understanding she
could barely tolerate. 'This helps no-one, Teya. Least of all
Perrin. It's night. They won't do anything until noon tomorrow
at the earliest. That's when the executions take place. Neri, get
the healer again. Then send food to the bedroom. And a city
map.'

'Why?'

Dallan glared over his shoulder at the jun. 'Because I said
so.'

'Dal, you know we don't have time for this,' the woman
said. 'You can't free him.'

Hope flooded Teya's body and she studied Dallan. He would help? Why? He must want something. What, though? His hands were warm and strong on her arms. She shuddered and moved out of reach. He let her go.

'Maybe we can't free him,' Dallan said to the jun, but he held Teya's gaze, 'but we can try. I can try, if you're not willing to help.'

'You'll undo all our plans for one nameless child's life?' The jun frowned at Teya.

'His name is Perrin!' Teya snarled. 'He may not have a colony funding-family name, like a jun, but he has a heart truer than every jun I've ever met.'

Dallan cocked his head. 'And I suspect you've met more than one, haven't you? Where are you from?'

She said nothing and shot him and Neri a suspicious look from beneath her lashes.

'Neri,' Dallan said. 'Just go.' He plucked at Teya's bloodied sleeve. 'And be quick.'

Neri spun on her heel, silk robes fluttering as she stalked along the hall.

'Neri, wait!' he called. 'Bring Ying Li. She's home on holidays, isn't she?'

The jun opened her eyes wide, nodded, and inspected Teya.

'Good,' he added. 'I think she'll be helpful in teaching control, don't you? Closer in age than anyone else in the city, too.'

Neri's doubt cleared. She nodded again and strode away without questioning him.

'Who are you to give orders to a jun like that?' Teya asked, eyeing him with wary respect.

He grinned and looked more like twenty-five than the thirty-something she had thought him. He patted the full purse at his hip.

'I'm the money in this venture. Quite a few juns are feeling the pinch at the moment.' The smile faded. 'They need me. The jundom needs me. And I need you, so they'll do what I ask—for now, anyway. Later…' He shrugged. 'That might be another matter. Come.' He tugged on her good arm. 'Let's get you fixed and fed. Then we can make plans about how to get Perrin.'

Pulling free, Teya folded her arms, hissing when the action hurt. 'What do you need me for? I'm just a kid, remember.' She might be fifteen, but people saw her as about twelve and that was a good thing. Adults underestimated children.

'No. You're not just a kid. You've got a gift. A gift you can use for more than petty theft, if you'll let me show you how.'

'No.' Her heart stuttered. 'You're wrong. I don't know what you mean. I'm nothing special.'

Sympathy lit Dallan's eyes. 'Yes, you are. You're xintou and we both know it.'

CHAPTER FIVE

DALLAN

Dallan observed the effect of his words on the girl-child. Her already-pale cheeks whitened to rival the oversized shirt she wore. Her sapphire eyes widened and darted left and right. He tightened his hold on her thin wrist.

'Come.' Her jerked his chin at the bedroom. 'You need rest. There's nothing to fear in being xintou. Most girls would be thrilled. It means a life of plenty and luxury.' He led her gently into the room and patted the bed. She hesitated and cast him a quick, half-frightened, half-defiant look.

'You're safe, Teya,' he assured her. 'You have nothing to fear from me.'

Her cheeks flushed. She clambered onto the bed and pressed her spine against the chimera-carved wooden bed-head. She pulled up her knees and dragged the heavy, embroidered quilt over them. He cleaned the spilt water and broken glass, waiting for her to speak.

'Xintou are Bonded to juns, aren't they?' Suspicion coloured her tone.

Interesting.

He kept his reply calm and light. 'That's right. They're telepaths and empaths. Telepathic Bonding helps them to better advise and control their jun. Each head of the twenty-one ruling jun families has one. From our Jun First, right through to the lowest Jun Sixth. Xintou are the reason the Jundom of Mamlakah has been peaceful for so long.' He scowled at the broken glass in his hands, trying to keep anger out of his voice. The situation in the jundom wasn't her fault.

'Others are Law Mistresses and advisors to the various House Masters and Mistresses. But they're all pledged to do whatever is needed to avert war between the juns, and between Mamlakah and the other Jundoms. The Xintou help protect us.'

'From who?'

Dallan chuckled. 'Ourselves, mostly.' He folded the glass in the wet linen and placed it on a table. 'Our ancestors came to Kalima to escape war on our homeworld, Earth. We're trying to avoid repeating past mistakes. The Xintou's job is to keep their jun in check so no one becomes too powerful.'

'But what if they don't?' Her voice sounded small and uncertain. 'What if they won't…when you…we need them to?' She crushed the quilt in her fists. 'What if they stand by and watch?'

Ah. Here was the ground to tread lightly over, then. Dallan sat on the bed's edge. Teya held her knees tighter to her chest, wary.

'Have you seen a jun do something unpleasant?' He waited. There. The flicker of revulsion and horror told the story even as she shook her head. He didn't press. Her reluctance to speak was understandable. After all, he claimed friendship with juns. He took another tack.

'Would you like to see a world in which the juns couldn't do such things to people you care about?'

Her eyes, full of guarded hope, flew to his. Then wariness shuttered their luminosity and she shrugged her good shoulder.

'That's not going to happen, is it? Not while they control everything. Besides…' Her face took on a cynicism far beyond her youth. 'If it's not the juns, it's someone else.' She studied him with dismaying frankness. 'There's always someone else to take their place.'

Time to tiptoe around that subject, perhaps. Dallan patted her foot through the cover. 'We need to concentrate on finding Perrin, eh?'

Teya aimed a haunted look out the window. 'Do you really think it's possible?' She plucked at the quilt. 'The last few weeks the junren-guards have been taking people every day and they never come back.' She swallowed. 'What if Perrin's already…'

'He'll be alright. I'll be honest with you, because I know you're tough and smart. The Jun First has required Jun Fourth Grey-Saud to lock Asalam under military control for her visit. She's afraid and Han Grey-Saud is stoking her fear. He wants to suppress what he calls "rebel elements" and he thinks clearing out the Migong slums will do it.'

'But Perrin's just a little boy!' she protested. 'And the Migongs aren't full of rebels, just people who are too poor to eat!'

'You and I know that,' Dallan said, 'but the junren don't. All they saw was a motley group attacking someone wealthy. That was enough.'

The small muscles in her jaw worked. 'What will they do to him?'

'Truthfully,' he said with a sigh, 'they'll either sell him to Melcor as a slave, or they'll execute him if no adult steps forward to prove his innocence.'

'Adult!'

He nodded. 'But don't look at me. It has to be a relative who can prove Perrin has no ties to the rebels the Jun First fears.'

'Couldn't you pretend?'

'Unfortunately, the Jun First and Jun Fourth both know me. I have a hunli ceremony partner. And together we have only one son—a little older than you—and no other living family. Not even any kin-children. I'm sorry.'

She deflated and hid her face against her knees.

'Don't lose hope, Teya.' The doorknob rattled. 'Ah, that'll be the healer. Enter!'

#

TEYA

Twenty minutes later, Teya teetered on the edge of unconsciousness, pain and fear dragging her into the abyss. The wound in her shoulder had been re-stitched by a healer who grumbled to himself about the stupidity of young girls and the inconvenience of being called out after dark.

He prodded at the old burn-scars on her back and asked who had botched the healing of them. She said nothing. He muttered a few choice oaths, but continued his stitchery with delicate care.

Teya bore his ministrations with gritted teeth, accepting a painkiller in the poultice over the wound, but refusing a sedative—unwilling to be drugged. No matter how kind Dallan seemed, he had a jun for a friend.

After the healer left, Dallan convinced her to eat some roast lu-deer a servant brought in. Hungry as she was, Teya waited until Dallan had sampled some, himself—which he did with irony. The meat was rich and flavoursome with herbs and salt. It had been years since she'd eaten meat so well-cooked and delicious.

'Have more.' He passed her the plate. 'Have you been alone for long? You and Perrin, I mean?'

'A while.' It was none of his business. She prodded her shoulder and winced. 'What was that thing the Migong hmar threw at me?'

He screwed up his nose. 'It's called a kpinga. A multi-bladed throwing knife of sorts.' He nibbled at another slice of meat. 'The slavers of Melcor use those and the kusarigama—

that spiked ball on a chain thing—to keep the slaves in line. Along with whips and an assortment of other niceties.'

Teya shivered. 'Whips.' She gazed out the window toward the darkened city. Somewhere out there, Perrin was being held, waiting, scared. Was he hurt? He was so little. She looked back to find Dallan staring gravely at her.

'We'll do everything we can, Teya. I promise. You can trust me.'

She shoved aside the food, suddenly ill and exhausted. Only Perring could be trusted. Everyone else was out to get what they could from her. Dallan wanted something. That must be why he'd rescued her this morning.

'Leave,' she said. 'And give me the key to the door.'

'You're in no danger here.' He glanced at the door. 'But before you fade away, I have one more surprise for you. Then you can have the key.'

CHAPTER SIX

TEYA

She pushed upright, yawned and forced her eyes open. 'What?'

'A friend,' he said. 'At least, someone I hope you'll come to see as a friend. Her name's Ying Li and she's close to your age. What are you, thirteen?'

'Fifteen,' Teya said. 'I don't need a friend. I need Perrin.'

'Ying's thirteen. And helping us get Perrin is why she's coming. Plus she'll stay tonight, so you feel safer.'

She curled a lip. 'Give me my dagger and I won't need a companion. Besides, what good is a little girl?'

'We'll see.'

A knock fell on the door. He opened it and beckoned. Curious in spite of herself, Teya waited. She'd left friendships behind five years ago when her mother vanished and left no-one else to care for Perrin. Staying in the village of her birth, north of Asalam had been impossible, so Teya had taken Perrin and hidden in a cart bound for Asalam. The first few days in the Migong slums had shown her the folly of expecting help or friendship. Everyone wanted something. Nothing was for free.

She watched with suspicion as Dallan bowed to a plump girl carrying a leather satchel and wearing a plain yellow house-robe. Ying, her round face and deep brown eyes alight with excitement and curiosity, bowed in return. She nibbled on the end of a lock of long, black hair, then flushed and tucked the hair behind her ear as though remembering instructions.

'Your hair is so pretty!' Ying blurted. Her blush deepened. 'I am sorry. Mistress Rua is forever telling me to hold my tongue.'

Dallan chuckled and handed her the large, bronze door key. 'I'll leave you two ladies to get acquainted. See you in the morning. Ying?' He tapped his temple and lifted his little finger.

There followed a moment of silence then Ying nodded and smiled sunnily.

'We'll be fine, Shenshi Johnston. We'll see you at breakfast. Goodnight.' She closed and locked the door then giggled. 'Now the olders are gone we can have some fun! I arrived from Madina two days ago for a…holiday.' She looked away, her mouth drooping. Then her cheerfulness returned.

'But Shunu Neri's family are all on her country estate so I've been *so* bored! You have no idea how nice it is to be out of the House! And to meet someone new. There's only thirty girls in the House and you get sick of seeing the same people every day. And I got in terrible trouble for telling on someone I thought had done something bad but she hadn't, so I got sent away for a few weeks.' She sighed. 'But I'm *determined* to be ever so good and I'll *never* doubt anyone from the House again. I mean, of course I should have known she wouldn't do anything bad. Everything the House teaches us is all about doing the right thing and being compassionate and wise and everything.'

She skipped around the enormous bed and dropped the bulging satchel on the floor.

Teya's eyes were heavy. There were nine Trade Houses in the Jundom of Mamlakah. They took on young boys and girls and trained them to be artists, or merchants, or weishi-bodyguards, or healers and such. But Ying hadn't mentioned which House she belonged to and Teya didn't want to seem like a zift by asking when she was clearly supposed to know.

Ying inspected the room. 'What a lovely room. Look!' She pointed at a tiny, polished-metal statue of the first colony ship, standing on the sandstone mantelpiece. 'Steel! Goodness.' She touched the object. 'Shunu Neri must be richer than I realised. She has an estate south of here, you know. It's quite small and plain. I lived there with my mother and went into the House in Madina when I was ten. I haven't been here before, though.

'I can never remember where all the twenty-one jun family estates are, can you? I wonder why Neri's in town when it's almost winter? Maybe because the Jun First is visiting. She has three children, you know? Neri, I mean, not the Jun First. She's only eighteen. But Neri's hunli ceremony partner is dead.'

Teya studied the younger girl in fascination as she chattered on about various jun families and their offspring and houses. Teya was so bemused, she didn't object when Ying clambered into the bed. Then Ying mentioned a name that broke the spell and Teya shivered.

'Han Grey-Saud,' Teya murmured, clutching at the blankets and staring into the darkness beyond the flickering mel-oil lamp. She curled a lip at Ying. 'You know him? You've met him?'

Ying screwed up her nose. 'Not exactly. I know *of* him and I've heard…things…about him.' She chewed her lip. 'We're not supposed to speak ill of the juns, but about a year ago I overheard Mistress Rua talking about him.' She gazed into the distance. 'She said he was too ambitious and ruthless. She thinks that, now he has a kin-child and jun-heir at last, the other juns need to depose him before he threatens the Jun First's throne.'

Teya stilled. 'He has a kin-child?'

Ying nodded vigorously. 'His hunlinna couldn't have children so he found a well-born woman willing to bear him a kin-child, evidently. A boy about three years old, now.'

'Willing…' Teya ground her teeth. 'And did anyone *ask* the woman if she was willing? Or did they turn a blind eye because he's a jun and can do anything.' Gray-Saud was the worst of them. The things he had done…Her back prickled with the ghost of old pain. She ruthlessly thrust aside memories as she had so often in the last five years.

Ying flinched. 'I…I…a jun wouldn't…he has a Bonded Xintou, Shana. She wouldn't allow him to…' She trailed off as Teya continued to stare coldly at her. 'I'm sorry. I talk too much. I didn't mean to upset you.' She touched Teya's arm tentatively. 'Forgive me.'

In the face of the girl's obvious distress, Teya melted. Exhaustion dragged her against the pillows.

'No,' she said, 'I know you didn't mean anything by it. It's been a gouri awful day and I'm tired.'

'Oh.' Ying stroked Teya's arm. 'Shenshi Johnston told me about your brother. I'm sorry I was prattling on about stupid things when you must be worried sick. I can help, you know?'

All her suspicions aroused again, Teya leaned away. 'How?'

Ying blinked innocently back. 'I can help you control your gifts, of course. I'm a xintou, too.'

CHAPTER SEVEN

TEYA

Teya threw aside the heavy covers, staggering as her feet hit the floor and exhaustion liquified her thighs. She rounded on the girl.

'Get out,' she said, low and hard. 'Get out and tell Dallan I'm done. If this is his idea of how to get my brother, then it's stupid and I'm not doing it.'

Ying gaped so Teya spun away and paced the huge room, prowling first into the darkened area at the other end, then returning to the yellow pool of light around the bed. She sent the young xintou a swift, assessing look, then stalked to the darkness again.

Flinging aside the curtain, she peered out the ground-floor window. She could climb out easily enough. Go find Perrin, herself.

To the southeast spiked the twin towers and upswept, peaked red roofs of Chinshi the Zah-Hill family's house. Next to it was the sharp black-tiled roofs of the Grey-Saud town residence. Where Han—when he visited Asalam—lived with his Bonded Xintou, Shana. She was like Ying and the other xintou girls who were trained to help and guide juns like Grey-Saud. Teya fought the urge to spit at both the jun's houses and turned away.

There had to be a way to get her brother and escape from Asalam. Away from xintou and jun, alike. Both were vile, vicious… she quashed the thoughts. Nothing could undo what had happened. Nothing could un-scar her back, erase the weeks of pain, or return her broken family to what it had been. Nothing would bring her mother home.

All she had left was Perrin. She had to find him.

Ying's dark eyes drowned in tears that spilled onto pink-flushed ivory cheeks and dripped unheeded to stain her yellow robe.

'Oh!' Her lower lip quivered. 'I'm so sorry. I had no idea.' Then her jaw hardened. 'No. I don't believe Shana would do that! You must tell Mistress Rua. She'll bring it to the Law Mistresses and they can find out the truth. It's not for you or me to accuse a Bonded Xintou of such things.'

Startled out of her anger, Teya paused. 'What? What are you talking about?'

Ying slithered from beneath the covers and hurried over. She stood before Teya, guileless and earnest.

'You must believe me. Xintou are not like that.' She held Teya's hands. 'They're good. Xintou House teaches us clarity, stability, responsibility, and compassion above all.' She crushed Teya's fingers between hers and Teya flinched. 'If Han Grey-Saud's Xintou, Shana, didn't stop Jun Gray-Saud from doing that to your poor mother—oh, and your house, and your poor back! Believe me, there's some mistake. You must have misunderstood.' She frowned. 'But maybe Mistress Rua, the Xintou House leader in Madina, *should* be told. No. Not without proof. Do you have any proof?'

Teya wrenched free and retreated. She clapped sweaty palms to her temples, staring at the smaller girl in horror.

'Did you…did you read what I was thinking?' Sickness dropped lead into her stomach and stones into her chest.

Ying nodded. 'Not on purpose. You don't have any mental wards. I couldn't read all of it, though. It's very jumbled. But I couldn't help it. You were thinking so loud and you hurt so much I couldn't block it out. I'm sorry.'

Teya quashed upwelling panic. It wouldn't help. This xintou was just a little girl. Not that big a threat. Yet. And perhaps there was information to be gained from her.

'Wards,' she said. 'Dallan could see me today when I faded myself, but his weishi couldn't. Would that have anything to do with these ward things?'

Ying nodded again, earnest. 'All juns and their families are taught to shield their thoughts, so the xintou bonded to other juns can't Read them. Shenshi Johnston grew up with Jun Neri's hunlin, so he learned, too. My mother should really teach you, because she's Jun Neri's Xintou. But she's at home on Jun Neri's estate, too close to birthing my gene-sister to travel. I can teach you, if you like!'

Teya cut her off with a chopping gesture of her good arm. 'I want nothing from you.' She turned to the window. 'I want out of here.'

To the east of the Chinshi, near the eastern city wall and barely visible even in the bright moonlight, stood the sandstone tower that housed the city junren and the small prison that served Asalam. Usually it housed fifty or a hundred prisoners.

Teya ground her teeth. Last report said there were over three hundred crammed into its dank space. But if Dallan was right, maybe the rumours were wrong and the inmates were being shipped off to Melcor as fast as the junren reeled them in. Was Perrin there? Terrified, perhaps beaten and abused by guards or inmates.

She had to find out. She couldn't sleep in comfort in a jun's house while he suffered.

She whirled to Ying, pinning the trembling girl with a sharp glare.

'Give me the door key.'

Ying hesitated then collected the key from a low table by the bed and passed it over. 'You can't go out. You're injured! And Neri's weishi and servants will see you. They'll stop you. It's too dangerous.'

Teya curled a lip. 'No, they won't.' The heavy key lay cold in her hand. 'I have to know where my brother is. I have to find out if he's alive.' She touched the hot, lumpy scar on her shoulder. It hurt, but not as badly as her back had, five years ago. She could bear it.

For Perrin she could bear anything.

Ying touched her arm, tentative. 'You're not well.' She rummaged through her bag, pulling out a cloak. 'Let me come with you.'

'No!' Teya pushed her away. 'No-one will care if something happens to me. But if you get hurt, I'll be blamed because I'm older and you're…important. You stay here.' She couldn't help the faint sneer. 'Where it's safe.'

Her lower lip pouting, Ying shrank. 'I'm xintou but I'm not a coward. I might not have seen as many horrible things as you, but that doesn't make you better.'

Teya sniffed. 'But it does make me less likely to get caught. Stay here. And don't tell. Promise?'

When Ying hesitated, Teya took a step closer. 'Promise or I'll jiche-well tie you and gag you.'

'You wouldn't!'

'Try me.'

Ying folded in on herself. 'Fine. But only if you promise to return—with or without Perrin.'

Teya scanned the warm room; the soft bed. She set her jaw. This was a jun's house. She couldn't afford to get too comfortable.

Ying straightened. 'Dallan promised he would help you. He's not a jun or a xintou. So you don't have to trust us, but you can rely on him. Besides, if you can't get Perrin by yourself, you'll need his help.'

'But what does he want? Nobody helps anyone for free.'

'You're wrong, you know. There are good people, too.'

'That doesn't answer my question.'

Ying's eyes fell. 'He didn't say. He does want your help, though. But he'd *never* force you to help. Ever.' Her hands clenched. 'And if he did, *I'd* stop him, myself!'

Against her will, Teya laughed at the image of the plump thirteen-year-old standing up to a skilled warrior like Dallan. But it was impossible not to admire her. The knot in Teya's stomach eased.

'Fine.' She took the cloak the xintou offered and awkwardly clasped it around her neck. 'I'll come back if I can't get Perrin out. Happy?'

'I guess. But you'll be careful? I'll wait by the servants' entrance and let you in.'

Sighing, Teya nodded. It was like having a mother all over again. But all the worst bits. The nagging and the guilt.

Together, the girls snuck along the darkened hallway of the Qin-Turner townhouse. Ying took the lead and tiptoed through a maze of interconnected rooms and hallways until Teya's head spun. Why would one woman even need a house this big? Fifty people could live here and hardly see each other. She barely resisted the urge to steal a silver cup someone had left sitting on a sideboard.

Ying laid a finger over her lips as they crept past a door edged by golden light. Voices murmured within. Teya waited, expecting an outcry. But only the sound of muffled, raised voices reached her. Sounded like Dallan and Neri. But the words were indistinct. Were they arguing about her? What did they want from her?

One thing was certain, if she got Perrin, she was *not* returning, promise or no promise. She buried that thought deep, in case Ying was listening.

On her way through the dark kitchen, Teya managed to collect a blackwood-handled ceramic kitchen knife. The scrape caused Ying to look around, but Teya stared, defiantly. Ying sighed and said nothing.

Outside the house, Ying peered around the cold, dark-shadowed courtyard.

She pointed and whispered, 'If you go through that little gate, the main street is a couple of blocks away. Go southeast until you get to the city wall—'

'I know where the east gate is,' Teya said. 'I know the city better than you do, xintou.' She ignored Ying's hurt little pout and strode for the gate. At the last minute, she looked back. Ying waited in the courtyard, a ghostly figure, drenched in moon-blood and shadows.

'Thanks,' Teya said, and slipped through the gate.

CHAPTER EIGHT

DALLAN

'You did what?' Dallan scrubbed at his face. 'Why? Why did you let her go?'

Ying Li stood before him in the library, chewing on a lock of hair. 'I had to. She said she'd tie and gag me! And he's her little brother.'

'You're a xintou, Ying. She has no wards, I assume?' Dallan waited for her headshake. 'You could have inserted the compulsion to stay.'

'I *couldn't*. How can you even suggest that? It's…it's…*wrong.*' She folded her arms and scowled at him.

Dallan grimaced. He'd forgotten how black and white children's thinking was. It had been so long since he'd seen his son. Months. Would Galric understand why his father was gone? What if he never made it home? Would the boy forgive him? He touched the Johnston family steel sword and dagger at his hip. He had to make it home to pass those on, if nothing else.

He shook his mind free of the pointless thoughts and considered the naïve xintou girl.

'You go to bed.' He rose. 'I'll go after her.'

'But I—'

He glared. 'Go.'

She huffed, but stalked from the room without speaking. Dallan hauled on his spice-otter-fur jacket, for the night was chill with autumn's bite. Stupid girl! Barefoot and wearing a shirt and a cloak. She was mad. Brave, but mad.

Why was she so desperate to get her brother, now, rather than waiting for morning? Why risk everything on a slim chance instead of getting help? What was she afraid of?

Could Perrin possibly be a male xintou? Cold sleeted across his skin. Surely not. Male xintou were forbidden by Xintou House. A danger to everyone around them once they reached puberty. But if Teya was a xintou, maybe her brother would be, too.

If that was the case, getting him out of Han Gray-Saud's control was even more important.

Frowning, he left the Qin-Turner house and wended his way toward the guardhouse, keeping to the shadows. Twice, the city junren passed close by, laughing, talking. One patrol passed a bottle of jiu back and forth, the liquor's sharp, clean smell cutting through the stink of horse manure and the lilac smoke from house hearths burning dried seaweed.

They were mighty relaxed for junren newly-placed under control of Han Gray-Saud. He was not one to appreciate laxness in his staff. If they returned to the guardhouse smelling of jiu they'd be in for an interesting lesson. Dallan waited for them to pass then ghosted through the quiet streets.

By the time he made it unseen to the guardhouse, the final curfew bell had pealed across the city, both moons were up, and the streets were deserted. He edged along the shadowed northern wall of a house and ducked beneath a window pouring golden light onto the cobblestones. Hidden in the darkest shade, he studied shadows around the guardhouse's bright-lit interior, across the little square.

Jiche! There. A slight movement of black against grey. Someone small and cloaked inching their way toward the front door. The girl couldn't be insane enough to walk right in?

She was too used to dealing with common folk. People who had not been raised around xintou. All juns and their close weishi were taught to ward their minds. The city junren commander was now Han Gray-Saud's chief weishi—his shangwei, Gennar Gen-kin. While Dallan didn't know him, the man was reputed to be a stickler for perfection and a strong advocate of both corporal and capital punishment for criminals of all kinds. He'd been known to beat a child to death for stealing fruit. His mind would be well-warded.

Dallan shuddered. He had to get to Teya before she tried to get inside.

#

TEYA

Teya crept closer to the door and paused, holding her breath so the puff of white wouldn't betray her presence. The two junren guarding the front door were standing to attention, not lounging against the stone wall or drinking as she'd seen them do in the past. She curled a lip. Gray-Saud's influence. On his estate, he punished his weishi for any wrongdoing. Real or imagined.

And if Gennar Gen-kin was still his shangwei, then she would have to be very careful. She had seen him only once. But once was enough.

Her shoulders twitched at the memory of heat and the stink of burning flesh. The crackle of burning thatch. Her fists bloodied from pounding on the solid door. Her throat raw from screaming.

She shook herself free of the swamp of dark memories.

Instead, she hunkered against the stone wall, soaking in what little remained of the day's heat while she waited. As soon as someone opened the door, she would sneak in and find a way to the cells.

Her injured right shoulder twinged. The painkillers the healer had put in the poultice were wearing off. The wound throbbed and her whole arm hung heavy, the fingers swollen. If it were her other arm, it wouldn't matter. But her left hand was clumsy when it came to theft and picking door locks. How would she get Perrin out of the cell? Could she steal a key, unseen?

She chewed her lip, uncertainty creeping in to displace the anger and fear that had carried her so far. A cold breeze caressed her legs and slipped beneath the cloak and shirt. Her feet ached and her toes were numb. The warm bed in the Qin-

Turner house held a strong pull. Maybe she could take Perrin there?

No. That was stupid-thinking. Dallan Johnston and Jun Qin-Turner wanted something from her. Putting herself and Perrin into their control would be madness. Whatever political games they were playing had nothing to do with her.

The guardhouse door latch clattered and the hinges creaked. A shaft of bright light speared the darkness. The two guards stiffened. The door opened further, emitting light and two heavily-cloaked junren heading out on patrol.

A tall, thickset man in Gray-Saud colours of copper and black emerged in their wake. He rubbed at his bald head and watched the two junren march south along the wide road.

He tapped the two door guards. 'You two are relieved. Get your replacements out here quick-smart. There's a lot of unrest in the city. I don't want this door unattended.'

'Bai, Shangwei Gen-Kin!' one guard snapped and hurried inside.

Gen-kin! Teya swallowed. No. She had to try. Now was her chance. She faded herself from view. She moved closer to the wedge of light, drawn like a nightwing insect to its promise. The shangwei looked her way and she stopped, blood thundering in her ears. No. He couldn't see her. She just needed to walk through the door while it stood open.

Two more paces and she would be in the light. But he wouldn't see her. No way.

She took one more stealthy step. A frown gathered on Gen-kin's sweat-slicked brow and he peered in her direction. He stirred, one hand dropping to the sword at his hip.

One more step. She gripped the kitchen-knife-handle in a damp palm. She could do this.

She moved into the light.

CHAPTER NINE

TEYA

Something grabbed at her left shoulder and jerked her into deeper shadow. A hand clamped over her mouth. Another wrenched the knife free. She stifled a scream, conscious of Gen-kin's closeness. A sharp kick backward missed her attacker's leg. Boots scuffed on the cobbles.

'There's someone there!' Gen-kin's rough voice pierced the silence and Teya stilled. Her attacker paused too. She tried to bite.

'It's me, you little zift.' Dallan's whisper brushed her ear. She sagged against him, her heart almost jumping out of her chest. She nodded and he released her.

'We have to get out of here,' he murmured.

'Get more men,' Gen-kin barked. 'There's someone there and I want them found. Now!'

The remaining junren at the door jumped and ran into the guardhouse. His alarm call echoed in the stone chambers and the clatter of footsteps followed his voice to the door.

'Gouri!' Teya growled. She ignored Dallan sprinted away, heading north to get off the main east-west road through the city. Light footfalls followed and she risked a quick glimpse behind.

Dallan. His hair and steel dagger gleamed in the moonlight. Behind him, torches flared at the guardhouse door. Burning with an ominous blood-crimson light.

She set her teeth and ran on.

#

DALLAN

Dallan caught up to her a block later. She was quick, even without shoes. Then she stumbled and cried out in pain. She leaned against a wall, clutching at her arm, one foot raised.

'I stood on something.' She offered the foot to him like an injured xiao-kitten.

He checked behind. The junren's cries and the flickering scarlet light of their torches danced off the surrounding walls. They weren't far away. He couldn't carry her to safety. Hopefully she hadn't trodden on anything that would cut too deep and leave a blood trail.

He sank onto his haunches to inspect her foot. She kicked at his chest, knocking him onto his rear. By the time he'd rolled over one shoulder and found his feet, she was half a block away. Her bare feet flashed in the moonlight. The cloak billowed behind her.

Ziftish brat! What was she thinking? Dallan scrubbed at his jaw. He should let her go. He had enough to worry about with the Jun First's visit and Gray-Saud's influence over her.

No. Teya was an unknown, which made her the perfect weapon in this war. He needed her gift. Until he'd met her, he hadn't been able to work out how to get close to Gray-Saud. Now he knew and he couldn't let her go.

Gaisi! He took off after her, just as the first junren rounded the corner behind. A shout went up and footsteps pounded the road. Fabulous.

Skidding around a corner, he glimpsed a ripple of cloth vanishing around the next and ploughed after her. She had doubled back and they weren't far from the Qin-Turner house now. Did she know it? Was she heading there? If so, why run from him? No, she would go to ground somewhere she felt safer. Where?

The Migong slums. That was her ground zero. A glass-rabbit-warren of twisting streets and alleys. If she made it that far he'd never find her.

Unless…

Ying! He wasn't a telepath. Male telepaths were forbidden. But he doubted the girl had gone to bed. Most likely she was listening out for Teya, so perhaps she would hear. *Ying! If you can hear me, you need to get Teya back to Qin-Turner house. It's vital. Please? I know you think it's wrong to manipulate her.* He paused, trying to work out how to convince her.

His lungs burned and his legs ached. He seemed to be outpacing the guards. Their cries had fallen into silence. But he'd also lost Teya. He halted in a narrow alley that stank of piss and vomit, listening. No sound of footfall. Had he passed her in the dark? Or taken a wrong turn? He surveyed the buildings around. Middle-class merchant and tradespeople's houses. Decent and clean. Not a lot of places to hide without being discovered.

Ying? We're being chased by the city junren and she's injured. If she hides we can't help her brother and she'll get sick of infection from that wound.

Fine. Her girlish voice sounded in his mind. *But I'll have to tell the Xintou House Mistress about Teya, you know.*

I understand. But right now we have to protect her. Thank you. He raised his wards again to hide the deeper, unspoken lie. No way was he letting Xintou House take Teya. Not yet. Maybe not ever, if she didn't want to go. He wasn't going to force her.

He waited, listening for sounds of pursuit past the drubbing of blood in his ears. Nothing, yet. He merged into the shadows and made his way toward the Qin-Turner house, glancing behind frequently.

#

TEYA

Teya staggered to a halt and sucked great gulps of air. She had to…catch her breath. She pressed at the stitch in her side and checked behind. Nothing. Neither the junren with their blood-torches nor Dallan with his stupid interference.

Oh! She'd been so close! She slumped against a brick wall, punching it with the flesh of her fist. The rough sandstone scraped her skin. Her chest tightened as she held in a scream of frustration.

A few more steps and she would have been inside the guardhouse. Why had he stopped her? Clearly her plans would have messed up his somehow. That must be it. He needed her so badly he had to make sure she didn't rescue Perrin, so he still had leverage.

Her fingers curled into claws. She should have known. He was friends with a jun, after all. Out for nothing but what they wanted. No care for the people they hurt in getting it.

She slid down the wall and curled into a ball, her forehead on her knees. The sobs in her chest tried to force their way out but she ground them between her teeth. There had to be a way. She couldn't leave Perrin in there. Couldn't let him be executed or sent into slavery. He was her only family. He needed her. She needed him.

Teya lifted her face and the cold breeze stung her eyes. Staring blankly along the grey-shadowed street, she chewed on her lip. What if…

She worked herself upright, using the wall, wincing. What if Ying Li could teach her to use her fading better? Not…xintou stuff like telepathy and messing with people's minds. But enough to help her fade from anyone—even people with wards like Dallan. If she'd been able to do that tonight, he wouldn't have found her.

Yes. She straightened. That might work. It wasn't yet midnight. She could learn that tonight and still have time to go get Perrin before dawn. In fact, it was better to get him in the early hours, when Gen-kin and most the junren were asleep.

Satisfied, Teya orientated herself. She wasn't too far from the Qin-Turner house. She must have run further west than she realised in her hurry to get away from Dallan. She could sneak in without him knowing.

She took off running again.

CHAPTER TEN

TEYA

By the time Teya eased in through the Qin-Turner's courtyard gate and arrived at the servants' entrance, her thighs were burning, her feet bruised and aching. Her right arm throbbed and stabbed slivers of pain through her chest. Nothing she couldn't handle and at least she had lost the junren.

The door opened as soon as she curled a fist to knock. She stumbled into the kitchen's gloom and sagged against the huge timber bench.

'Little zift,' a deep voice said.

She sagged, too tired to protest when Dallan slipped his arms under her and carried her upstairs. She cried out when he laid her on the bed and unlaced the shirt to reveal the bandaged kpinga-blade injury. She batted at him.

'Stop it, you zift,' he said. 'I'm checking you didn't tear the stitches again.'

Ying hovered nearby, tears shimmering on her lashes. 'Oh, I *knew* you shouldn't have gone without me.'

Dallan silenced her with a look and peeled aside the bamboo-cloth bandage. He inspected the injury, smeared on a thick cream smelling sharply of tea tree and re-tied the binding.

'No stitches burst this time. You were lucky. Twice tonight.'

Teya glared. 'I was almost inside. *You* stopped me. I'd have Perrin out by now if you hadn't.' She struggled up in the too-soft bed and slumped against the carved wooden bedhead. 'I won't do it!'

Dallan's smile was weary. 'Won't do what?'

'Whatever you want me to. I know you stopped me so I'd have to help you.'

He swiped at his disarrayed hair and sank on to bed-edge. 'I stopped you because Gen-kin has been trained to ward his mind. He would have seen you, as I could.'

Teya said nothing. Was he telling the truth?

'Think about it,' he continued. 'Gen-kin is the shangwei for Han Grey-Saud. Who knows a jun's security weaknesses better than his chief weishi? Most juns train their closest weishi to ward. Grey-Saud has more to hide than most. The second you moved into the light you'd have been caught. You'd be in a cell with Perrin right now.'

'At least we'd be together,' she muttered.

'And either executed or sent off to Melcor as slaves, tomorrow.'

A long silence fell, broken only by the crackling of burning seaweed bricks in the hearth.

Teya lay on her left side. 'Go away. I'm tired.'

The mattress shifted and Dallan's footsteps faded toward the door. 'I'll send breakfast in early for you. We have a lot to do in the morning if you want to save him.'

She didn't reply, fighting to keep captive a cry of despair. She wouldn't give him the satisfaction of knowing he had her where he wanted her. The door lock clicked and Ying's bare feet slapped on the timber floor. The bed bounced as she clambered in and snuggled under the covers.

'You must be exhausted,' Ying whispered. 'Get under the quilt and get warm. Morning will bring light into darkness.'

'Morning brings hunger and someone else trying to take what you fought to hold onto yesterday.'

Ying's cold fingers crept into hers. 'It doesn't have to be that way.'

'For you, maybe.' Teya pulled free. 'You told him where I was going, didn't you?'

Long lashes veiled Ying's eyes and her cheeks grew rosy. 'I had to. I was so worried. And I'm glad I did. He's right. Gen-kin would know how to ward. Your gift only works on those without wards. You'd have been caught.'

Teya sat up, swallowing when the room spun. 'Then teach me how to ward and how to get *through* their wards.'

Ying chewed on a lock of hair. 'But it's forbidden. A non-xintou can't tell when you push through their wards. It's one of our strictest rules of etiquette.'

'I'm not of Xintou House. I don't care about your etiquette. If I'm going to get Perrin, I need to fade so *no-one* can see me.'

Doubt shadowed Ying. Teya changed tack. The girl had been well-drilled in Xintou morality. She wouldn't go against her House Mistress without a strong reason. What would make her? Ahhhh…

Teya forced her thoughts onto Perrin, picturing his maimed foot, his mischievous giggle; his sparkling eyes and dirt-smudged gaunt cheeks; indomitable; innocent. She let the despair and fear she'd buried well up until it lodged in her chest and blurred the room. She dwelled on how lost and lonely he must be, how afraid, how young, how alone.

He was her only family now; her reason for continuing the daily struggle to live. She opened her darkest thoughts, focussing on the agony of losing him and the pointlessness of life without him.

Ying threw her plump arms around Teya's waist. 'Oh, please, don't,' she whispered. 'I'll help.' She sniffed, gazing at Teya through eyes of drowned darkness. 'We'll start now. I can teach you to ward so…'

'So I'm not so loud?' Teya suppressed a flare of triumph.

'I'm sorry,' Ying murmured. 'I've never felt such pain. I'm so sorry.' She touched Teya's scarred back. 'I'm sorry.'

Teya pulled away. 'You've led a sheltered life, then.' She pointed at the window. 'There's a lot of it out there, where I come from.'

Ying slid out of bed, settled in a padded armchair and folded her legs, tucking her long nightgown under her feet. She straightened her spine.

'Very well.' She gestured to another chair. 'Sit and let's begin.'

Teya dropped into the seat.

'The teachers at the House always say creating wards is a bit like building a wall.' Ying centred on Teya. 'But I always think of it more like gentle hands cupped around my thoughts, hugging me.' She gave herself a hug as though to demonstrate.

Teya sent her a dry look. 'The wall sounds good to me. So I just build one? All round? Even the top and bottom?'

Ying nodded with a patient little smile. 'It will take practice. And you need two walls. One around your innermost secret thoughts. And one that protects your Outers – the thoughts you don't mind sharing with others sometimes.'

Teya pictured two walls. One deep in her mind and another growing inside her skull, between her brain and the bone. Something light but strong. Alzin, perhaps—the aluminium alloy that weishi wore as body armour. When she was done, she opened her eyes and found Ying gaping at her.

'I can't read you now,' the xintou whispered.

'That's good, isn't it?'

'Yes…but…' She nibbled on her hair then spat it out. 'Fine. Let me try to get through. You might feel like something's poking at you. If you do, re-inforce that part of your ward to stop me.'

There, a nudge against the outer alzin wall. Teya thickened it and filled in a hairline crack. And another. She bared her teeth as the prodding grew harder and more cracks appeared. She filled them as fast as Ying created them.

A Future, Forged p75

Finally, Ying sagged in her chair, panting. 'Wasai! I can't get through your wards. I mean, I only learned how a few months ago, but still. How do you do it?'

Teya permitted herself a smile of satisfaction. 'Maybe I have better reason to need strong wards than your House sisters. This is important to me.'

Ying cast her a dubious look.

Teya touched her temple. 'So how do I make sure they stay, even when I'm asleep. And I can't spend every waking minute thinking about wards.'

'You don't have to. We don't really understand it, but there's something instinctive in a xintou's mind when it comes to wards. It's harder for non-xintou. They have to rethink their wards two or three times a day. If they forget, it's easier to break them. But once I've tried to get through a few more times, your mind will understand and they'll stay without you having to do much.'

Cocking her head, Teya asked, 'Can I try getting through your wards?'

The younger girl shrugged, confident again. 'Sure. But you have to relax…' she let out a long, slow sigh '…and open your heart. Xintou must always use their gifts from a place of love and compassion and trust. Anger and fear will make it more difficult to access your powers.'

Teya sneered faintly. Anger helped her get through each day. Anger at Han. Anger at his Xintou. Anger at a world that let people like them do horrible things without justice. It gave her strength to keep going. Compassion was wasted on people like that. And trusting people was plain stupid.

But she breathed slow and deep, just in case. It couldn't hurt. She wasn't angry now, anyway. Determined, though. This would be a useful skill against Gray-Saud and his pet Xintou.

She extended a thought. Ying's wards looked like they were made of that volcanic glass…obsidian. That was the name. Shiny, black, brittle-looking.

Teya considered. The surface was smooth. Not a crack or a flaw. So maybe, if she couldn't pry it open, she could smash it? She pictured a hammer of steel, solid and heavy. She swung it hard into the obsidian. A crack appeared.

Ying jumped and squeaked. A thrill screwed through Teya's stomach. She inserted a steel dagger into the crack and twisted. The gap widened. Ying uttered a little scream, her eyes stark.

Teya drove the dagger-thought through her ward and into her Outers. Not far beneath lay a second layer of obsidian. This was easy. She smashed the hammer against that. Ying whimpered as cracks appeared. Teya pried at them, picturing doing the same thing to Shana's wards. How wonderful it would be to see that woman squirm.

'Stop! Stop! Please,' Ying whispered, her face a rictus of agony. 'Oh, please? If you break through my Inners we'll be in danger of Fusion. We could both die.'

Teya hesitated, steel thought-dagger poised. She had a xintou at her mercy. She'd be doing everyone a favour by killing her.

CHAPTER ELEVEN

TEYA

Teya withdrew her thoughts and checked her alzin wards were solid. Ying huddled in her chair, eyes glistening with tears, arms wrapped around her soft body.

Swallowing a surge of guilt, Teya patted her shoulder, but Ying flinched away.

'Sorry,' Teya muttered.

Ying peeked out, still curled in a tight ball as if that would protect her mind.

Teya shifted in her chair and scuffed the bamboo floor with her bare toes. 'I'm really sorry, Ying. I didn't mean to scare you. I was imaginging breaking Shana's wards.'

The xintou stayed silent, sniffling. Then she rubbed at her nose.

'No,' she said, her jaw set. 'You scared me, but you also showed me my wards are weak. It's never been my best skill. The House mistress who teaches it always rolls her eyes at me. So teach me to do what you do. Then I can put yours to the test—and strengthen mine.' She nodded. 'What did you picture? What were you thinking and feeling?'

Teya hesitated. Did she want to give away her methods? Well, the xintou was genuinely trying to help.

'I was feeling…excited.' It sounded wrong to say it out loud. Especially after Ying's instructions about compassion and trust.

'Well, that's better than anger, anyway.'

'And I pictured a hammer. Made of steel.'

Ying's jaw dropped. 'Maybe that's it. Xintou House mistresses teach ways that are less painful for the receiver. And not many people think about using steel—I guess because it's so rare and doesn't come to mind.'

'What does the House teach?'

'Imagining you're dissolving the ward with weak acid. It takes longer, though.'

'Acid's less painful? Your mistresses are nasty.'

Ying snorted a giggle then became serious. 'Be careful. Fusion isn't the only risk. Xintou work is exhausting but it sneaks up on you. I've seen girls faint and fall into comas for days because they forgot to rest and eat.'

Teya rolled her eyes. Soft, pathetic girls, maybe. Resting and eating had been luxuries for the last five years.

It took another hour before Ying was satisfied both of them had the strongest wards possible. Teya was still able to break through Ying's outers, but not easily or quickly. Every time she got frustrated, Teya found the hammer harder to picture. It faded into insubstantial nothing.

Maybe there was something to Ying's instructions about keeping her anger under control. She'd have to think about it. Anger had sustained her this long. She'd never considered letting it go. Not until Gray-Saud was dead.

Ying could not break Teya's wards at all—which pleased Teya, though she hid it from Ying. Whether a more experienced xintou would be able to penetrate them was impossible to know. Ying had only been at Xintou House for three years. At least it meant Teya had some protection against Shana, next time they met.

By the time they climbed into bed, both girls were yawning and snippy. Teya's eyes were sand and her mind mud. Her stomach rumbled but there was only water to drink. Not the first time she'd gone to sleep hungry.

She sank into a storm of nightmares in which Han Grey-Saud took her instead of her mother, heedless of Perrin's protests; in which Perrin's decapitated head adorned the spear of Grey-Saud's weishi as her mother watched in disinterest and nursed her new son.

Teya awoke to the pink of dawn with salt-tears crusting her cheeks and the sheets crushed between her fists.

#

TEYA

A knock sounded on the door and Teya padded across the room to unlock the brass latch. Dallan swung into the room, followed by a servant bearing a tray laden with food. When the servant departed, Dallan joined them at the breakfast table.

Ying, tousle-haired and heavy-eyed, yawned, groaned and rolled over in bed.

'Up you get, Ying,' Dallan said, pouring himself a cup of pale blue lancha tea. He offered the pot to Teya, who poured a cup, ladled in three teaspoons of honey and sniffed the aroma in appreciation. Then she poured pink gidfruit juice into a heavy green glass and sipped while Dallan dumped pastries and scrambled eggs onto her plate.

Ying dragged herself, grumbling, out of bed and slumped in a chair, staring vaguely at the food. Teya poured the girl a cup of lancha tea and winced. Her shoulder had stiffened in the night and hurt more than ever.

Dallan pointed at her injury. 'Make sure you move it. Keep the muscles warm but don't tear the stitches again.'

Teya bit down the impulse to say he wasn't her father and to stop telling her what to do. She cocked her head. Time for an experiment. She slowed her pulse and prodded at his wards as Ying had taught, searching for a weakness.

There: a slim crack in his concentration. She inserted a wedge and used her steel hammer to drive it deep. His wards crackled and split. A wave of dizziness blurred her vision. She gritted her teeth and pried his Outers open. Then she faded herself from his sight.

'Gaisi!' Dallan's cup fell from his grasp and smashed on the timber floor, spraying hot lancha tea onto his blue silk trous. He swore again and dabbed at the liquid with a napkin, scooping up the broken crockery.

Teya relaxed her thought and hid a smile behind slurping her tea. Her hand trembled but the honey would restore her strength.

He visibly regathered his composure and turned thoughtfulness on her. 'That was…impressive. You're a quick learner. And skilled if you got through my wards so easily. I'm glad Ying was able to help you control your gift.'

Ying sat up straighter, beaming.

'Remember,' he added, 'I couldn't feel that, but a xintou will. Use your gift with care. Any other abilities I should know about?'

Teya and Ying both shook their heads.

'She doesn't seem to have any of the usual xintou gifts: telepathy, empathy, or even foreseeing,' Ying said, nibbling on a sweet bun. 'She can *hear* words if I put them into her mind, and I can hear her replies. But she can't reach out to my mind and start a telepathic conversation. It's very strange. She's good at warding, though. And at getting through wards. She finds even the tiniest crack. But she's terrible at controlling her emotions.'

Teya glared and Ying offered an apologetic smile.

'But otherwise,' Ying added, 'she only has that ability to cast illusions.'

'Illusions?' Dallan's attention sharpened on Teya. 'Can you show someone more than your own invisibility?'

'I...I don't know,' she lied. Flames and screams. A woman's cry for help. A door smashing open. She shuddered.

Ying chewed her hair. 'I guess you could send any picture you like. Sort of like telepathy, but without words.'

'Try,' Dallan said. 'Show me my teacup, full and intact on the table.'

'She shouldn't do too much, shenshi,' Ying said, earnest. 'We were up late and she hasn't eaten yet. You know how tiring xintou work can be.'

He sighed. 'Of course.'

'Don't mother me, Ying. I'm a big girl.' Teya studied her own cup—a thin-walled thing of delicate beauty, translucent and painted with geometric patterns in grey and copper. It had been a long time since she'd tried anything but her own invisibility. Concentrating, she created an image and drilled it into the crack in Dallan's mind.

He laughed. 'Oh, well *done!* That is incredible.'

The room darkened and tilted. Teya clutched the cup with weak fingers. She fought the urge to vomit and forced herself upright in the chair.

With a wondering expression, Dallan reached for the imaginary cup and waved through empty air. 'Wasai!'

Teya dropped the image. A fluttery tension in her chest confused her for a moment until she identified the feeling: pride. Something she hadn't felt for over five years; the desire to have someone's good opinion; the relieved thrill of praise. She clenched her jaw and replaced her cup on the table with more force than needed. The crockery clattered in the silence.

Ying jumped and blinked sleepily. 'You should eat, Teya. You're so pale.'

Teya ignored her, folding her arms to hide the shakes. She considered Dallan.

'What, exactly, do you want from me? And how are you going to help me get Perrin?'

'Excellent questions,' he replied, stretching his legs beneath the table.

'Then you'd best give me some excellent answers,' she snapped. 'It's already morning and I've wasted too much time with tea and mind-games.'

'I want your help.' He paused and inspected Ying. 'Ying, how much are you in your mother's confidence?'

Ying smothered a yawn. 'I don't know, shenshi.' She assumed an air of haughty dignity that contrasted oddly with her mussed hair and sleep-wrinkled robe. 'But my loyalty lies with Shunu Neri Qin-Turner, since I'll be her next Bonded Xintou after my mother retires.' Her cheeks flushed. 'As long as I don't do anything silly again.'

He smiled. 'Yes, Neri told me you'd falsely accused a senior student of something and that's why you've been sent away for a few weeks.'

'Oh, I learned my lesson. I'll *always* make sure I have proof before I say *anything* bad about *anyone*. And I should have known a xintou wouldn't do something terrible.'

Teya said nothing. The girl was naïve and as brainwashed as the rest of Mamlakah's people. Everyone believed xintou were untouchably perfect.

A Future, Forged p87

'What about your loyalty to your House?' Dallan asked.

The girl's dignified certainty faded. 'Why? Are you planning something with Jun Neri and my mother that Mistress Rua would disapprove of?'

'It depends,' he hedged. 'Do you know how she feels about Jun Fourth Grey-Saud?'

Ying repeated the conversation she'd overheard from Mistress Rua and Dallan's doubt segued to grim satisfaction.

'In that case, no, I don't think Mistress Rua would disapprove.' He hooked his hands behind his head. 'Han Grey-Saud has too much influence. I suspect he's…' He slid Teya and Ying a sidelong glance. 'Well, Jun First Jenna Zah-Hill is young and impressionable. She's only eighteen and with her parents dead, she lacks reliable guidance. She's also the first female Jun First for over a hundred years, and many of the male lower juns are making noises about whether a woman can do the job.'

Teya snorted and Ying glowered.

Dallan held up a hand. 'I have no qualms with a woman running the jundom—as long as she's competent. I certainly wouldn't want to. The problem is, Jenna admires Han Grey-Saud when she shouldn't.'

'What are you saying?' Teya frowned.

'We need to get rid of Han Grey-Saud,' Dallan said, 'and you're the one who's best positioned to help me achieve that.'

CHAPTER TWELVE

TEYA

A knock fell on the door and it opened to admit Shunu Neri Qin-Turner, regal in a heavy grey robe with copper edging around the hems. A broad-shouldered, xiao-bear of a weishi followed and took a watchful stance behind her chair when she settled beside Dallan.

The woman smiled gracefully. 'Good morning, girls, Dallan. Don't let Barrod and me interrupt your breakfast.'

Teya glowered at the jun. She scanned Neri's stoic shangwei, Barrod. With his stern jaw and sharp black eyes, he seemed to see everything. He stood now in a corner of the room, one hand on the hilt of his ceramic sword, the other on his dagger. His gaze skimmed across hers without changing expression. Arrogant. Just like his mistress.

Dallan bowed and spread honey on a pastry. 'We were discussing how Teya might help us with our Gray-Saud problem.'

Neri scanned Teya, faintly scornful. 'I don't see how. We need to deal strongly with him and she's hardly—'

'Don't.' Dallan cut across Shunu Neri's objections. Her eyes glittered but she shut her teeth with a snap.

Teya studied him. He was only a first-family. Money or not, how could he speak so boldly to a jun?

'Don't be disrespectful, Neri. And don't underestimate her,' Dallan said. 'I agree we need to kill him. But we haven't got the manpower for an assault on Grey-Saud, and a paid contract to the xiongshou-assassins of Weishi House would be traced to us. You know how scrupulous they are about paperwork. Besides, Mistress Keyli of Madina Weishi House works closely with Mistress Rua of Xintou House on political assassinations. They only happen if both approve. And, while I think Rua approves in theory, if I'm wrong, and she feels keeping Grey-Saud alive is better for the jundom, she'll have to take action against us.' He eyed Neri sardonically. 'Do you want your Xintou turned against you?'

Next to Teya, Ying paled. 'Mother wouldn't!' She sent a shocked glance at Neri.

Neri sighed. 'She would, child. And she would be within her rights. It's the House's duty to do what they deem necessary to keep peace and stability in the jundom. If they feel a jun is becoming too powerful, they can replace him or her with the next successor. It's the way of things for the last four hundred years.'

'So why haven't they replaced Grey-Saud, or his Xintou, then?' Teya snapped.

Dallan sent her a look of mingled sympathy and uncertainty. 'I'd like to know the answer to that, myself. Any thoughts, Ying?'

The young girl wrapped an air of dignified authority about herself. 'I can only guess, shenshi.' She shot a quick, half-scared peek at Teya. 'But given…other things I've heard of Gray-Saud and his Xintou, Shana, it's possible she could have turned against the House to side with him for some gain to herself. But I don't believe it. Not without proof,' she finished.

Neri stiffened. 'Turned! How could she?'

'It happens sometimes.' Ying nibbled on a pastry. 'But it shouldn't. Xintou House is meant to keep Mamlakah stable and peaceful. It shakes the peoples' faith in us when this happens. We must get evidence. Then we can tell Mistress Rua.'

'My word isn't good enough, I suppose,' Teya said.

'Unfortunately,' Dallan said, 'no. Unless you want the Law Mistresses reading you and your memories very closely. Do you?'

Teya hunched a shoulder.

'We should send a message to Mistress Rua,' Neri said.

'Agreed.' Dallan lifted a finger when Ying straightened. 'But not quite yet, if you don't mind? His smile became nasty. 'There are a few other things we need to have ready before Grey-Saud's stripped of his Xintou and his title.'

'Like what,' Teya asked, fascinated.

'Like his successor.'

'But Ying said he has…a son.' She swallowed the acid that rose with the words.

'Yes,' he agreed, 'but he's a child and would need a regent. Too young to be Bonded to a xintou, either.'

A Future, Forged p91

'And Shana's gene-daughter should be the next Bonded Xintou for the family,' Ying put in. 'But she's only eleven. So either the Grey-Saud family would have no Xintou until she's older, or the House must appoint a new one and that would be unfair. She was genetically crafted for that role.'

'So was her mother,' Teya muttered. 'But being born a xintou doesn't make you a good person.'

Ying flinched. 'No, but most of us *are* good. It's not fair to judge all xintou by the actions of one. Especially when we can't prove anything.'

Teya studied the younger girl but held her tongue.

Neri ran a hand over her mouth. 'Who did you have in mind for Grey-Saud's successor if not his son? You set a dangerous precedent if you don't put a direct heir in his place, even if the heir is kin-child, not full-blood.'

Dallan's grim smile returned. 'But doesn't the law state that a kin-child who is the product of a forced union, is not eligible to be heir?'

'Forced!' Neri blanched. 'Is there evidence?'

He eyed Teya.

Her cheeks washed with heat as unwanted memories flooded in. She was there again. In the fire. Choking on smoke. Screams. Hers. Blistering pain. Also hers. Her body curled protectively around baby Perrin.

Her heart skittered and sweat prickled beneath her arms. She dragged in slow breaths and struggled to keep her new mental wards in place. When she was in control, she shot Ying a glare. The young xintou must have told Dallan.

'Only what I saw,' Teya replied, her voice cracking. 'He took my mother and his Xintou watched on.'

Neri spread her hands wide. 'An appalling act, to be sure, but how do we know it's the same woman?'

Teya clenched the chair arms, but said nothing.

'What's your family name, Teya,' Dallan asked.

Something lodged in her throat, closing it with an iron fist. She forced herself to relax.

'Connor,' she murmured, stroking the gold locket at her breast.

'And the woman he has used to father his kin-child heir is named Helva Connor.'

'Yes,' Teya grated, 'that's my mother. She was midwife to his first hunlinna but the baby was stillborn and a girl. Han was so angry he wouldn't let my mother treat his hunlinna, so the poor woman bled to death. He told everyone she died in childbirth. He blamed my mother. Destroyed her reputation. Then, when she had no income and no friends and no other choice, she had to accept his offer to bear his kin-child. He had been pressuring her for years.'

'Why her?' Dallan frowned.

Teya inspected her hands, twisting in her lap, glad of her new mental wards. 'She never said.'

He sat back, mouth bitter. 'It's typical of Han to choose a woman from a well-known first-family to bear his kin-child. He thinks those without first-family or jun names are lesser beings. I'm surprised he didn't bind her in the hunli ceremony, but the woman he did take as a second hunlinna is a jun's daughter—which he would think a better political choice.' His scowl deepened. 'But where's your father in all this? Surely he must have objected to your mother's change in situation.'

Teya stared blindly out the window, into the brilliant green sky. Her chest ached, her throat ached. Everything in her mind and body ached with tight-leashed pain and anger, years old but nonetheless potent and sharp.

'Dead,' she spat. 'Or as good as. He's nothing to me or Perrin.'

Dallan studied her for a long moment before sitting forward again.

'Is Perrin likely to tell the city junren his family name?' He sipped at a fresh cup of lancha tea and observed Teya over the rim.

She shrugged again. 'Don't know. Maybe. We left the Grey-Saud estates when he was a baby, but I told him all the stories my mother told me, so he knows. It doesn't come up much. In the Migongs no-one cares who you are.'

'Well,' he said, 'in Grey-Saud's prison, they will.'

CHAPTER THIRTEEN

TEYA

Teya tried to ignore the squirming sickness in her gut. 'Why should the prison guards care what Perrin's family name is?' If they found out the truth, what would they do to him?

Dallan placed his cup on the table with deliberate care. 'I've heard rumours that prisoners from good families are being separated. Ransomed back.'

Neri gasped. 'That's…monstrous! How could the Jun First allow such a thing? And the Law Mistresses—don't they read prisoners to determine guilt or innocence? They'd recognise the boy's situation and protect him.'

Teya bit on a fingernail. Perrin might be innocent of attacking Dallan, but he was guilty of many minor crimes and a xintou would read that and condemn him anyway. What did they care about a little boy?

As he scratched at his scalp, dust flew from Dallan's dark hair and skittered restlessly in a beam of orange sunlight. 'That's the problem. I don't think Han and Shana are allowing the Law Mistresses access. And I have a horrible feeling Jenna doesn't know. Madina is a long way from here.'

He cocked his head. 'Or Han has convinced her it's another way to raise much-needed revenue for the Crown. Not unlike the way he's campaigning for legalisation of slavery.'

Teya gulped. She'd heard rumours about the Melcori slave-trade. About the conditions on the boats going downriver to Melcor. The end of year death-games slaves were sent to if they tried to escape. She shivered.

Neri rubbed at the arms of her chair. 'I still don't believe Jenna will legalise slave ownership in Mamlakah, no matter what Han advises. She'll listen to the Council of Juns.'

Dallan shrugged. 'The juns are struggling financially. You know that. And the Melcor economy is booming since they legalised slavery. If you don't have to pay your workers, you can produce goods and food much cheaper. They're selling live runiu herdbeasts, and bamboo to Adhegal, Mamlakah, and even south to Jadid, at half the price of what we can charge. Mamlakah estates bordering on Melcor lands have started using slaves.

'It's only a matter of time before it spreads. Jenna is anxious to prove herself fit to rule, so she doesn't want to hear about the negatives.' He scowled. 'At least, not from me.'

'Well.' Neri shook her head confidently, but her fingers trembled as she picked up her cup. 'I think you're worrying too much. I don't think Jenna can possibly know what's going on—with Melcor or with Gray-Saud holding hostages for ransom. She's young, but she's not stupid.'

Dallan raised bleak eyes to hers. 'But her Xintou hasn't been seen in weeks, from what I hear. Where is she in all of this? Why isn't she guiding Jenna?'

Ying's mouth dropped open. 'Didn't you know? The Jun First's Xintou is sick with something Healer House can't diagnose.' When Dallan raised his brows at her, she flushed. 'I overheard Mistress Rua telling another Mistress.'

'Interesting.' He scratched at his jaw. 'Worrying. I may have underestimated Han. If he has…arranged this illness then Jenna may be in greater danger than I thought. Without her Xintou's protection, she could be influenced by Han's Xintou, Shana.'

Neri scowled. 'No. Jenna would have strong wards. The Jun First family is always taught by the best.'

'Shana wouldn't do such a thing,' Ying stated, only to shrink beneath Dallan's weary regard.

He sighed. 'Then why is Han taking his hostages out of the main prison and holding them in the cells beneath the Chinshi? Not even Jenna could be that blind. And he's staying in guest-quarters in the Chinshi, too.'

Time stopped and ice congealed Teya's blood. 'Perrin's in the Chinshi?' she whispered. 'It's impossible to get in there.'

'We don't know, yet, child.' Neri touched her wrist and Teya snatched her arm away.

'Don't gouri touch me, *jun,*' Teya snarled, half-rising. 'I'm not a child. I stopped being one the day Han took my mother and left me and Perrin for dead in a burning house.'

In the corner, the weishi, Barrod, shifted. His dark gaze fixed on Teya and she sank back into her chair. Typical jun. Couldn't fight her own battles.

She turned on Dallan. 'If we're going after Han Gray-Saud, I'm in. What do you want me to do?'

'I can get you into the Chinshi.' Dallan drew his steel dagger from its sheath and laid it on the table. 'Then you'll sneak into Han Gray-Saud's room and kill him. With this. And I'll make sure Perrin is free and you're reunited with your mother. Safe on my family estates outside of Asalam. You'll never want for anything.'

'You can't send a child to do something like that!' Neri protested.

Dallan silenced her with chill consideration. 'Teya said she's not a child. I agree. She deserves the right to revenge her mother.'

'That's *not* how things work,' Neri replied. 'We have a law system for a reason.'

'Well,' he said, 'the law system is broken and the man who broke it isn't likely to step aside without a fight.'

Teya studied the dagger with longing. The steel blade was sharp, gleaming, but the yanstone in the pommel seemed dull and white instead of glittering with light as they were supposed to be. How odd.

'What do you get out of it?' she asked.

'A chance to talk sense into the Jun First without Han around to twist her thinking,' Dallan said. 'If we can't influence Jenna, people like you and Perrin will be slaves before the year's out and those gouri kusarigama and kpinga will be in the hands of every jun and slavemaster.'

Teya shifted, her shoulder twingeing. 'And if I get caught?'

He neither flinched nor gave anything away. 'I'll deny I know you.'

Ying caught her breath and Neri frowned.

But Teya nodded. She'd assumed that was what he'd do, but hadn't expected the honesty. She held up the dagger. 'And I suppose I've stolen this?'

His mouth curved up. 'You catch on fast.'

'Why this dagger, though,' Teya asked. 'Mine would work.'

Dallan's face blanked. 'There are reasons.' He retrieved the dagger and slapped the blade lightly into his palm, his expression faintly contemptuous. 'One of which is that Han wears an alzin chest plate under his robe at all times. Your bronze blade wouldn't go through it.'

He'd said 'reasons', but only stated one. Teya waited but he remained silent. What was the other?

Neri grabbed Dallan's arm. 'You can't, Dal. She's not a xiongshou.'

His gaze remained on Teya. 'She doesn't need to be a trained assassin. All she needs to do is get close enough to stick this into Han's heart.'

'How on Kalima is she supposed to do that? The Chinshi is guarded night and day by dozens of weishi and junren loyal to the Zah-Hill family. You and I can't even get in without an escort and an appointment.'

'She can do it.'

Neri inspected Teya. 'Dallan, she's too yo—'

Teya shot to her feet, fists clenched. Her legs shook. She should have eaten.

'You call me a child one more time, *jun*, and I'll…' She laid a hand on her hip, but Dallan had not yet returned her dagger. She smiled thinly. Perhaps there was a better way. 'No, I won't. You will.'

She drove her thoughts against the jun's smooth wards but the hammer slipped and bounced off, leaving them unbroken. What? What was wrong? She hit again, harder, heat boiling from deep within. The steel hammer in her mind glowed the dull red of hot metal.

Still nothing. No sound. No shattering of those grey, featureless wards.

Shaken, Teya hesitated. What was she doing wrong? It had worked so well against Ying and Dallan. What was different?

Neri produced a condescending smile. 'Child, you need to rest. You're overwrought. Dallan and I will think on it some more. We'll come up with something, don't you fret.'

Teya glowered, biting off another angry retort.

Neri picked up half of Dallan's broken teacup. 'What happened here? This was my good set. Ow!' Blood welled from her fingertip.

A crack appeared in her mental wards.

p100

Teya concentrated on the slim fissure. The room swayed and darkened. She steadied herself with the chair back and sucked a calming breath. Too late to eat, now. She could prove her point and do it after. Neri needed to be taught a lesson.

A blow with the steel hammer of her thoughts and the crack widened. Her ears rang with a distant, discordant song. Another blow and the crack in Neri's ward became a chasm.

Teya stiffened her knees and swallowed nausea. Now the woman would see.

Neri screamed.

CHAPTER FOURTEEN

TEYA

Shunu Neri leapt from her chair, batting at her arms and hair. 'Put it out! Put it out! Help me, Dallan! Barrod!'

Teya smiled in satisfaction.

'Teya! Enough.' Dallan shook Neri. 'Stop, Neri. It's not real. It's not real. Tighten your Outer wards. Do it!'

Barrod rushed forward, sword half-drawn, glowering uncertainly at Teya.

The jun struggled in Dallan's arms, crying piteously and trying to slap at her hair and arms.

A cold hand gripped Teya's wrist.

'Tey,' Ying said, her voice a squeak. 'Stop it, please? It's not Neri you're mad at. She's nice. Really.'

Teya met Ying's pleading look and rode a surge of shame. Perrin would be horrified, too. She let go the illusion and hunched her shoulder. The room surged and flowed like the hotsprings water through the town's pipes. She shook her head and blinked to clear it.

'Neri, you're alright,' Dallan assured her.

The jun stood trembling. She turned her hands over and over, her cheeks pale and sweating. Then she nodded shakily and smoothed her unmarked robe. Dallan and Neri both looked to Teya. Him frowning, Neri fearful.

Barrod advanced, bulky, black-clad, infinitely more menacing than the jun.

Teya shrank away. She had attacked a jun. She must be mad. The door was too far away and she still wore an oversized shirt, without other clothes or weapons. She was in the power of these people and they wanted to use her for their own ends. What would they do now they knew she was dangerous?

'Wh–what did she do to me?' Neri said. Barrod stalked closer, his sword out.

The chair caught Teya behind the legs and her knees collapsed. Every muscle shook and her bones liquified. She could barely lift her arm. Faces blurred. Voices were distant echoes, heard down a tunnel.

Ying shifted, putting herself between the weishi and Teya.

'Don't hurt her! It was an illusion.'

Teya felt the younger girl shaking and regarded her in bleary wonder.

'Illusion?' Neri checked her arm and patted her clothing, her expression bewildered. 'But the flames…they felt so real. So hot. I could smell the skin and hair burning.'

'She's scared of you, Shunu Neri.' Tears glistened on Ying's lashes. 'The things Jun Grey-Saud did to her family…' Her voice broke.

'Ying,' Teya said, the skin on her back crawling at the memory of pain. 'I don't need protecting. I can look after myself.' She struggled to her feet, put the younger girl aside and stared at Neri defiantly.

But the strength of irritation lasted only a moment and the room pitched again. She dropped to her chair and closed her eyes, hoping the room would stop spinning.

'Here.' Ying offered a sticky sweet-bun. 'Eat. You've done too much. Eat it!'

Teya shoved the bun in, chewed and swallowed. Her stomach rebelled, but she forced the food down. Ying was right. She had overestimated her strength and that couldn't happen again. Not if she wanted to get Perrin free. She ate another bun and guzzled a glass of the too-sweet gidfruit juice, ignoring the weishi who still hovered close by.

Strength seeped into her limbs, golden and warm.

After a long, thick silence, Neri sat heavily, staring at Teya. She waved Barrod aside and the weishi took up his watchful stance a few steps away, his attention fixed on Teya.

'It was so real,' Neri whispered, switching to Dallan. He nodded.

'And I think that's our ticket to get close to Han.' He considered Teya. 'Do you think you can trick more than one person at a time? Like you faded yourself from my weishi? I'll relax my wards to make it easier.'

Teya perched on the edge of her seat, nibbling on a redberry pastry. 'Don't know. It's a bit different when it's not just hiding myself.'

'Don't overtax yourself!' Ying said. 'And be calm. Open. That will make it stronger.'

Waving a dismissive hand, Teya projected an image of Perrin into Dallan's mind. Dallan started and considered the empty space next to her chair.

'Your brother. Hard to believe he's not here. Neri, open your wards so she can try showing you.'

The jun stilled, then nodded and held herself rigid. Teya grimaced, trying to seem like she was concentrating. She already knew she could put an image into the thoughts of five people at once. No need for the jun to know that.

Neri shook her head. 'I can't see anything.'

Teya slumped in her seat. 'I guess not, then.' The room spun but no way would she admit weakness. She drank more juice, trying to hide the shaking of her arm.

'Disappointing,' Dallan said, scratching at his jaw. 'But not the end of the world. We'll get you a robe suitable for a Chinshi servant. That will make you practically invisible once you're inside. It's finding a way to get you inside that's the trick.'

A soft knock fell on the door and Neri called out, 'Enter.'

A servant entered, dressed in severely-cut dark grey robes with copper detailing. He bowed and passed over a rolled piece of bamboo paper. 'Message for you, shunu. Urgent from the Chinshi.'

'Is the Messenger House runner who brought it waiting for a reply?' Neri traced the blue wax seal with a fingertip.

'No, shunu.'

'Dismissed.'

p106

He bowed and retreated, closing the door. Neri broke the seal and unrolled the soft paper. She scanned the message, and swore softly.

'We may not have time to experiment, Dal. I asked Hassien to message me if anything unusual happened in the Chinshi.'

Dallan nodded. 'Good. That was the whole reason you gifted his contract to Jenna on her adult Nameday ceremony three months ago. A jiaoji-lover has better access to the Jun First than anyone else. We were lucky Hassien was willing to help. What does he say?'

Teya listened. She had considered applying to Jiaoji House, herself. Jiaoji were well-respected and the House taught all manner of useful skills, beyond the arts of seduction. They were picky about their students, though, taking the most intelligent and preferring those who were physically perfect. Her scars would have excluded her. Besides, she couldn't have left Perrin to fend for himself.

'He hasn't had much time with Jenna,' Neri said. 'Said she was polite enough, but didn't seem to be interested in him.' She gave a small, wry smile. 'I think he was offended. After all, he was by far the best student out of Jiaoji House for his graduating year. He thought perhaps she was interested in women.'

'But?' Dallan prompted.

Neri tapped the roll of paper. 'I think we now know why she wasn't interested in Hassien. Han Gray-Saud's second hunlinna has died in an accident and he has proposed to Jenna.'

The jun's pale eyes were bleak. 'Jenna accepted. The hunli ceremony that will bind them—and put Han on the throne as consort—is set for tomorrow.'

CHAPTER FIFTEEN

TEYA

'Khara!' Dallan rose and paced to the window. 'He moves fast. *That's* why he invited her to visit Asalam. He wanted her out of Madina. Away from Mistress Rua at Xintou House. Away from the Jun Council. An accident.' He spun back. 'Does it say what sort of accident? Is there a way of proving Han's involvement in his hunlinna's death?'

Teya scowled. Of course Han had killed his hunlinna. It didn't need to be proved. He'd done the same to his first, letting her die from bloodloss then acting all broken-hearted. Everyone in Asalam knew it. But his Xintou hadn't turned him over to the Law Mistresses for that crime, either.

'Hassien doesn't say any more about that.' Neri read the scroll again. 'Only that Han's hunlinna was on the Gray-Saud estates, not in Asalam. But there's no doubt he's consolidating power. I did hear rumours Han intends to pledge his younger sister to Jun Second Alric Koh-Lin.'

Dallan made a noise of frustration. 'Of course. Alric's not yet eighteen and his mother is Han's cousin.' He sat and dropped his head into his palms. 'I'm a shazi, Neri. I should have seen this coming. Han's been planning this for years. He'll control of two of the three major jundoms.'

Neri nodded. 'And the other Jun Second, Carval Ma-Safra, is fifty-seven with no heir yet. His youngest kin-brother, Qidan Ma-Safra, has been Han's lover for years. Every time Han is in Madina they're practically joined at the hip. Undoubtedly, Han promised Qidan the Jun Second's title in exchange for support.'

Teya waited, jiggling one leg. The welter of names and titles made little sense.

But Ying whispered, 'And with the Jun First and both Jun Seconds in his control, Han could legalise slavery straight away.'

'Not only that,' Dallan said. 'He already owns some of the largest rattleberry silk farms. If he runs the whole jundom, he could expand south into Jidad and take control of the massive herds of snow-deer and the yar-pine plantations Prince Fahad's family have been nurturing these last several decades. Or north into Adhegal to control the bamboo plantations.'

Teya growled. 'None of this matters. Who cares what Adhegal grows or where yar-pine comes from?' She rose and held her aching right arm with her left. 'I want Perrin. Enough talking. Get me into the Chinshi so I can do what needs doing.'

Dallan shook his head. 'No, you're in no condition to take on Han. He trained in Asalam Weishi House for several years as a young man. I thought we'd have a few days for your injury to heal. Or we could get a nai-xintou to help.' He eyed Ying askance.

p110

'Sorry, shenshi.' Her return look held guilt. 'I'm not nai-xintou. Micro-telekinesis is rare. There are three with the gift at the moment and they're all out in other towns, attending to Bonded Xintou who are ready to fertilise their eggs and genetically engineer their gene-daughters.'

'Not your fault.' Dallan grimaced.

There was a long silence until Ying spoke timidly. 'What about Mistress Rua? Can she help? She must know what's going on.'

'Han thought of that, too,' Dallan said. 'A flitter-bird message arrived this morning from my sources in Madina. Mistress Rua left Madina two days ago to attend an emergency mediation between two juns disputing land allocations in Jiali, to the east. She'll be well out of telepathic range of even the strongest Xintou House mistress. By the time she gets a flitter-bird message—assuming she ever gets one—and returns to Madina, the hunli ceremony between Han and Jenna will be done.'

He growled. 'I can't believe he caught me so offguard. I thought we'd have more time to plan before he moved.'

Teya glared. 'What *was* your plan before you met me?'

He shrugged. 'I was going to try killing him, myself. I trained at Weishi. The same time as Han.'

'And did you ever beat him in a fight?'

Dallan emitted a reluctant laugh. 'No. And we haven't seen eye to eye for a long time. He never lets me near without his weishi close by. He's not stupid.'

'So we don't have any choice,' Teya said. 'Once Gray-Saud is on the throne, your precious Jun First will last less time than his first and second hunli partners did. He'll kill her, declare himself Jun First and make his kin-son the new Jun-Heir.'

'You're not ready,' Dallan said. 'Casting illusions in a safe room or against people in the street with no wards is one thing. Going into the Chinshi and up against people like Han when you're under pressure and frightened is another.'

'I've done it before,' Teya said bitterly. 'And been frightened every day of my life since I was ten. It's never stopped me from using my gift.'

He laid a hand on her injured shoulder. 'Did you use it yesterday when that Migong mob attacked us?'

'Well, no, but—'

'That's what I mean.' He tapped his temple. 'When you're scared, logical thought goes out the window. You need food and healing. Plus time to practice breaking wards and throwing illusions under pressure. Otherwise you won't be able to when you're panicking or angry.' He regarded Ying, who nodded. 'And I know Ying has told you xintou gifts work better when you're calm and open.'

Teya rose and stalked around the room, touching things blindly. He was right, of course. She knew how hard it was to cast an image when she was scared. But what choices were there? And it wasn't his decision to make. He and Ying and Neri had no authority over her. Nor did they have to be there,

p112

in the room, knife-in-hand. The blood would, literally, be on her hands.

And if she were caught, Dallan would disavow her. As would Ying. Of course they would. Dallan had a family to protect. Ying had a career ahead of her and a jun to shield.

Unaccountably, tears blurred the room and Teya had to take a deep breath to fill the sudden emptiness in her chest. She was just tired, still. That was all. She could do this. She'd been hoping—these last five years—for a chance like this.

She returned to the table. 'We don't *have* time for training and practice. I'm fine. I've eaten. And I *have* done it under pressure before.'

Flames, screams, pain, anger. Such rage.

She lifted her chin. 'Get me that uniform. We need to go. Today. I'm not taking the chance that Perrin might get murdered or sold to slavery. Take me now or I'll go on my own.'

CHAPTER SIXTEEN

DALLAN

'Stop fidgeting,' Dallan muttered. 'You sure you're alright? Did you eat enough?'

One step behind him, Teya stopped twisting the hem of her black-and-silver Zah-Hill servants' tunic, thrust her hands into the sleeves and swore at him. Dallan repressed a laugh. The girl had guts, he had to give her that.

If only he could be certain of her loyalty and her ability to handle the stress. She was the linchpin of a very shaky plan and she was untried, her aims entirely on retrieving her brother. If this failed there might not be another chance.

But she was right. There was no time to spare.

'Fade yourself,' he said as they approached the Chinshi's enormous front gates of timber and iron. 'And stay out of sight of one of the guards so you only have to trick one at a time.'

She huffed a faint laugh but shifted beside him so the guard on the door's northern side couldn't see her. The one five feet away ignored her.

Dallan addressed him. 'I'm here to see Han Gray-Saud. Tell him Dallan Johnston wishes to see him.'

The weishi raked him with a cold, sneering inspection. He rapped on the gate and the smaller door, inset into the larger, creaked open. The weishi passed on the message and Dallan stepped through, with Teya close by. She shuffled around keeping Dallan's larger body between her and one of the two guards inside. The weishi ignored her and waved Dallan into the main entrance.

Dallan surveyed the twin bloodsandstone towers that dominated either side of the courtyard. Three hundred years they'd stood. Asalam was the second-oldest city on Kalima. A monument to the tenacity and vision of the colonists who'd left Earth in search of an ideal world with freedom for everyone.

He set his jaw. Their dream had been realised for five hundred years. No power-hungry despot was going to destroy it. Not if he could help it.

Once they were inside the central building set between the towers, Dallan relaxed a fraction. Now Teya would blend in and she'd only have to cast illusions once she got close to Han.

He guided her into an alcove beneath the sweeping staircase and bent to catch her eye.

'Right. Now it's up to you.'

She dragged her awed gaze away from the huge steel sculpture of a colony ship that dominated the entrance to the Chinshi palace proper. Her cheeks were pale. One hand rested on the Johnston steel dagger, sheathed at her hip, beneath the tunic. Her fingers flexed, so tight on the handle their tips turned white.

'It's ok, Teya.' He tried to sound reassuring. 'You can do this. I'm going down to the prison cells and see if I can find Perrin.'

'How will you get him out?'

He lifted one foot. 'Lockpicks in the heel of my boot. Old trick I learned from my father, who was a bit of a rogue.'

Teya raised a dubious brow but said nothing.

'Here. Take this and go that way.' Thrusting a roll of bamboo paper into her hand, he directed her toward the stairs. 'Act like you belong. Head high. Shoulders back. Ask the first servant you see where Han Gray-Saud is. Tell them you have a message to deliver in person. They won't question you because of the uniform. When you find him, hide until he's on his own.'

He quashed doubt. This had to work. 'Then kill him, hide the knife under your uniform and run out of his room, screaming for help. Once the chaos starts, get out, ditch the uniform and make your way home.'

'You mean the Qin-Turner house?' Her lip curled. 'That's not my home.'

Dallan sighed. 'Sorry. Yes.'

'You *promise* you're going to get Perrin out?'

'I promise.' The ticking of boots on stone made him glance around. 'Go. Before anyone comes.' When he looked back she was gone. He waved through the place she had been, but it was empty.

He turned to the southern tower. The prisons were in the base. Question was, what excuse did he use to see who was in there?

TEYA

Teya retreated from Dallan and faded herself. He checked where she had been, then marched toward a door beside a massive tapestry covered in strange, unrecognisable animals. Should she follow him, to make sure? She hesitated, then ghosted in his wake. He rapped on the door and spoke to the weishi behind it.

'I'm here to see one of the prisoners,' he said, his tone haughty and bored.

'No admittance by order of the Jun First,' the weishi said.

'I have her permission.'

The weishi considered Dallan for a long, harrowing moment. Teya held her breath in as the men confronted each other, neither backing down. He wasn't going to let Dallan in.

CHAPTER SEVENTEEN

TEYA

She settled her heart, stretched out a thought and found his wards. Nowhere near as strong as Neri's or even Ying's. Easy. She wormed an illusion into a crack in his ward. Now he saw a note in Dallan's hand. An order to allow entry.

The weishi started, frowned, then shifted aside, opening the door. 'Five minutes.'

Dallan vanished within and Teya let out a huff. He was a hmar. How would he have gotten in without her? He probably would have left and said he couldn't. That would be typical.

She stalked away, holding the steel dagger still tucked beneath her tunic. It didn't matter. Once she killed Han Gray-Saud, she could get Perrin herself and get out of here. Maybe her mother, too. Her breath hitched. Would her mother even remember her? Did she still care? Or had the new baby replaced both her children in her love?

Teya found her steps faltering and paused halfway up the grand staircase. She'd been so focussed on finding Perrin and killing Han she'd never considered the possibility of seeing her mother again. Helva Connor probably thought both her children were dead in the fire lit by Gennar Gen-kin on the day Gray-Saud kidnapped her. Of course she must.

Would she be happy, surrounded by luxury like this? Teya took in the impressive, vaulted timber ceilings, the blood-red walls of the towers at either end of the foyer, the rich smells of timber polish and roasting meat, the sound of distant laughter and music from somewhere upstairs.

It was a far cry from the two-roomed cottage where Helva Connor had raised Teya and birthed Perrin. A far cry from the hand-to-mouth existence of a woman scorned by the village for—

Teya stopped the thought cold. No point in rehashing the past. She was here to correct the present and free Perrin.

Dagger handle tight in her grip, she took the stairs two at a time.

#

TEYA

A servant directed her to a room on the south tower's third floor. Teya sucked a slow breath, trying to calm the drubbing of her blood. She climbed the broad spiral staircase, each step harder than the last. Her palms grew sweaty and slipped on the smooth timber railing.

She reached Han's door and hesitated, trembling. No. She pulled back her shoulders. She could do this. Remembering all the reasons she hated this man helped. Bitter heat billowed from deep inside, driving away fear. She clenched her teeth.

With the fake message crushed in her right hand, she knocked with her left and waited.

The door jerked open. Teya froze. Gennar Gen-kin glowered at her, one hand on the door, one on his sword. Too late to change her image in his thoughts. He stared right at her.

He couldn't recognise her. She'd only been in the light for a second last night. Maybe he hadn't even seen her? And she'd always hidden from him, back in her home village—though of course he knew she existed. But even on that last day, he couldn't have seen her. Not with all the smoke and fire. He thought her dead. They all did.

His expression didn't change from bored and cold. She relaxed a little. No. He didn't recognise her.

'Message?'

She nodded. 'Private. For Shenshi Gray-Saud.' Her voice quivered and broke.

'Bring it in, then.'

Teya forced her feet to move through the treacle trapping them. Inside the apartment she tried to keep calm and pretend everything was normal. A Chinshi servant wouldn't be astonished by the luxury, but it was hard to ignore.

Heavy, dark-wood furniture dominated the room. A massive dining table and eight ornately-carved chairs. A chandelier of actual blackened steel, fitted with real electric bulbs hung overhead. The red-timber floor was covered by huge silk rugs in abstract designs of black and silver. And, set into the northern wall, a large window of stained glass threw beautifully-coloured light across a broad, wooden desk.

Standing beside the desk was a tall, lean man with dark red-brown hair. His back was to her and she stretched a thought out to test his wards. She needed to find a crack. The surface was hard and smooth. Solid. Not even a hairline fissure. She concentrated and forced her roiling blood to calm.

Then she pictured the steel hammer she'd used to break Ying's wards.

The man turned and pierced her with eyes the colour of storm clouds.

'Ah. Who have we here, Gen?'

Behind her, the shangwei grunted. 'Yes, shenshi. It's the right one.'

Han's smile broadened and he rubbed his palms together. 'Excellent. Come. Sit, boy. I've been expecting you.'

CHAPTER EIGHTEEN

TEYA

Teya jumped. 'I…I don't understand, shenshi.' She thrust the message at him, her hand shaking. 'I'm just delivering a message.' Her heart thudded, fear replacing anger. Her thoughts scattered. She couldn't focus well enough to pierce his wards and fade herself. Certainly not well enough to trick both men at once.

She was a shazi. She should have prepared better. Waited for the door to open rather than knocking. Slipped in unseen. What had she been thinking? She hadn't. She'd been arrogant and angry and stupid. Now she had no choice but to try and make this work. Somehow.

Han strolled over and accepted the message, his smile condescending. Teya waited, trying not to shrink from his piercing scrutiny. He couldn't recognise her. He'd only seen her twice in her life. Once as a child and once had been through the haze of her burning house. Five years before. She'd changed a lot since then. Surely…

He tapped the message roll and walked in a circle around her. 'Message from who?'

'Dunno, shenshi,' she managed. 'Took it from the Messenger House runner at the gate.'

'So, not from Dallan Johnston, then?'

She controlled a twitch of reaction. 'Dunno, shenshi.' She forced out the scripted words Dallan had written for her. 'Can I take the runner an answer?'

'Oh...' He threw the message onto the desk and sauntered over to her '...yes. But maybe not the one Johnston was expecting.'

'I...I don't understand,' she repeated. She needed to centre. Needed to get into his mind. She swept a tentative thought over the smooth surface of Han's wards. They were rock hard and solid. Stronger than Ying's or even Neri or Dallan's. She readied the hammer in her mind. This wouldn't be quick or easy.

The hammer faded, slippery and insubstantial. What? What was wrong with her? Oh. Anger. She had to get her emotions under control.

But the fire in her gut bubbled too hot at the sight of Gray-Saud's conceit. He deserved to be smashed to pieces physically as well as mentally.

Teya curled her fingers into fists. She could do this. She concentrated again. The hammer re-emerged in her mind.

A real ceramic sword appeared by her ear and all thought of casting illusions vanished. Her stomach knotted. What should she do? Run? There was nowhere to hide. Gen-kin loomed beside her, his blade caressing her neck. He chuckled.

'Saw your face, boy. Last night.' He leaned closer, his breath rank. 'Thought you lost my men when you ran, didn't you? But they followed you. All the way to the Qin-Turner house. With Johnston. Now.' He dragged a dining chair into the middle of the room and pointed at it. 'You're going to sit while Shenshi Han explains a few things.'

Her legs shook so much Teya could barely move. She stumbled to the chair and sank into it. If she could *think*, she could get herself out of this. She could do this! Had to. Hot and cold sleeted across her skin.

Han rotated a chair and straddled it, resting his arms on the back. He tilted his head.

'You seem…familiar, boy. Do I know you? You're not a Chinshi servant, I know that. One of Qin-Turner's servants? Or Johnston's?'

She shook her head and repressed a shaky sigh. He still thought her a boy. If he realised she wasn't, though…

'Whatever Johnston has offered you,' he said, 'I'll double it.'

Teya gasped. 'What?'

'You heard me.' His cool expression didn't change. 'Whatever he offered you to kill me, I'll double it if you kill him, instead.'

'I don't…he didn't…' She stopped. That was too close to an admission.

Han waved her words away. 'Let's lay our cards on the table, shall we? I know Johnston wants me dead. And I want him in a similar state. He's an interfering hundan.' He sniffed.

'He doesn't understand what I'm trying to do. Our economy can't continue as it has.'

His regard returned to her. 'Where are you from, boy?'

Teya swallowed. 'The Migong slums, shenshi.'

'Then you know how poor our people have become. The Melcor way of binding the poorest people to the rich simply means they are always assured of a meal and a place to sleep and work to do each day.'

He threw out his arms. 'Why can't people like Dallan Johnston understand that? It's not about taking away people's freedom, it's about making sure everyone has the basics and the rich provide for the poor.'

He smiled. 'So mothers don't have to sacrifice for their children. Older siblings don't have to sacrifice for their younger ones. You understand, don't you?'

She understood sacrifice, alright, but… Teya said nothing. Could Dallan have got it wrong? What if Han wasn't intending to enslave unwilling people at all? What if all of this was because of a misunderstanding? There was no denying that many people in the Migongs would be better off if what Han said was true.

She shook herself. Was she mad? He couldn't be believed. She, of all people, knew that.

Han sighed. 'But Dallan won't listen to reason. Xintou House won't approve an assassination and he's too well-guarded for an illegal attempt. So.' He slapped the chair timber. 'That leaves you, boy.'

'Me?' Teya forced her voice into lower registers. 'I'm not going to kill him for you.' With the immediate threat of a sword through the throat withdrawn, her mind was clearing, though her limbs still shook with the aftermath.

Han rose and crouched before her. Now was her moment. Her hand crept to the dagger under her tunic. She prepared the hammer's image again, ready to strike at his wards and push an illusion into his mind. To distract him.

She grasped the dagger.

Something yanked her arm. She cried out. Gen wrenched her wrist painfully and the knife fell to the floor. He released her, gathered the dagger and passed it to Han. Teya cradled her wrist, rubbing at the red marks left by Gen's fingers.

Han inspected Dallan's steel blade. 'Yes, I recognise this. I'm not surprised he wanted you to use this. Did he tell you why?'

Teya shook her head.

He barked a laugh. 'Again, I am singularly unsurprised. He always was a coward who let other people do his dirty work.'

Han took a few steps away, then came back. He crouched again and searched her face, tapping the steel point on her thigh. She tried to control the shaking of her hands and stare at him insolently. But she couldn't stand against his intensity.

'If you kill him, I'll give you anything you want,' he said. 'Anything you can think of.'

She hesitated. 'Anything?'

He tucked the dagger into his belt. 'Within reason.'

A Future, Forged p129

She could ask for Perrin's freedom. This would be over. They could leave Asalam. Go south to Shanzhai, maybe. Away from all this madness.

Could it be that easy?

'Han?' A woman's voice broke into the silence.

'Shenshi?' A second woman's voice followed, deeper, stronger.

Teya and Han both turned toward the sound. The bedroom door framed two women, one tall, deep-chested, wearing the traditional shimmering gold robes and half-veil of a Bonded Xintou

Teya's fists curled. Shana Blake, Han's Xintou.

The woman's eyes were obscured by the translucent gold half-veil, but she gave a grunt of what might be surprise.

The second person was a small woman of about thirty-five, her long, dark hair loose past her shoulders, a blond toddler on one hip.

Her sapphire eyes widened.

'Teya!'

CHAPTER NINETEEN

TEYA

'Teya?' Han shot to his feet. 'Gouri!' He held her chin and turned her to the light. 'Of course. I'm a shazi not to have seen it.'

He gestured to Gen-kin and nodded toward Teya's mother, who was hurrying across the room. 'Get Helva out of here.'

Gen-kin wrapped an arm around Helva's waist and hauled her away.

'Mother!' 'No!' Teya and her mother spoke at once. The toddler wailed. Teya half-rose from the chair, but Han's iron hand pushed her down. His thumb dug into the knife-wound and her knees collapsed with the pain. She let out a whimper and rode a surge of nausea.

'Shana,' Han said, 'get a message to the weishi in the cellblock. I want that boy.'

The Xintou nodded and her gaze unfocussed. 'Done, shenshi. Shall I stay while you interrogate her?'

Teya felt a sharp prodding at her wards. She stiffened but kept her expression blank. The Xintou was trying to break through.

Shana's mouth pinched at the corners. 'Strong wards. It would take time, but once they're gone she'll do what you want.'

Han gestured indifferently. 'No need. Keep Helva quiet and get that boy.'

Gen-kin hauled Helva from the room, silencing her tearful calls with a ringing slap. The child let out a cry, cut off by the slam of a door. Voices murmured, words indistinguishable. Gen-kin reappeared. He locked the bedroom door, then the exit, leaning against it with his muscular arms folded and coldness curling his lips.

Pinned to the chair by Han's unwavering examination, Teya shrank in on herself, cursing her stupidity. She should never have agreed to this. Dallan had been right: she wasn't ready.

Han strolled around the room, surveying her. 'I suspect I know what motivated you to help Dallan.'

She said nothing, fixated on her fists clenched in her lap.

'Gen tells me there's a boy in the southern tower prison cells who claims the name of Connor. Perrin Connor, in fact.'

Teya couldn't help a quick glance at him. The smug expression there made her stomach drop.

He shrugged. 'I thought it a lie or a co-incidence, but it's not, is it? You both survived. How is that? Gen burnt that hovel to the ground.'

She ground her fingers together until they were numb. There had to be some way to use her gift. Some illusion she could throw into his mind to distract him. She played with wild ideas of fire and her own imaginary death, but could think of no way to wrest the door key from Gen-kin without betraying the illusion.

There had to be something she could do! She had to *think*.

'There is something you can do,' Han said.

Teya blinked at him.

'Kill Dallan and I'll release Perrin. I'll even set you up in your own house. Perhaps find you a hunlin.' His lips warped into a smug smile. 'Yes, in a year or so, when you've filled out, I could use you to good advantage somewhere.'

She shuddered.

He laughed softly. 'Do we have a deal?'

What choice did she have? She nodded, hating the frisson of guilt that twisted sickness in her gut.

'Excellent,' Han said.

'Give me the dagger,' she managed. 'Or he'll guess.'

He patted the blade where it lay tucked in his belt. 'No, I think I'll keep this as a souvenir. Gen, do you have that phial of gu-spider poison I asked you to get from Weishi House Poisons Master? Give it to her.'

The shangwei sauntered over and thrust a small ceramic phial at her. Dark blue and stoppered with wax, it looked innocuous. But gu-spider venom was lethal, even in small doses. Even Teya knew that. She stared at it, then took the phial and dropped it into a pocket without speaking.

'Go, then, girl,' Han said. 'You have one day. I want to hear his death cried on the streets by the Messenger House runners by this time tomorrow. If I don't, then Perrin dies…no.' He flashed white teeth in a mirthless smile. 'He'll become the first of my slaves in the new economy. He's a pretty enough boy, I hear. I'm sure my friends will quite enjoy his…company.'

Gen held the door open and laughed.

Teya staggered from the room. Tears blurred the long, dark hallway and she almost missed her footing on the winding staircase in her haste to put distance between them. The phial bumped against her leg with every step.

At the bottom of the stairs she paused, lost, trying not to vomit her horror.

'Keep walking,' Dallan's voice hissed from behind her. 'Head up. Walk as though you're on an important errand. When we're outside the gates we'll talk.'

Her legs boneless and mind scattered, Teya could think of nothing else to do but obey.

CHAPTER TWENTY

DALLAN

Dallan studied Teya, debating how to approach her. She hadn't spoken a word the whole way from the Chinshi. Now, back in her bedroom, she sat curled in one of Neri's plush armchairs. Her knees were drawn up to her forehead, her good arm around her legs as though they were a shield.

'What happened?' he asked, dropping into another chair with a heavy sigh. 'I'm guessing you weren't able to kill him?'

Teya said nothing.

'Where's my dagger? You—'

The door burst open and Ying rushed in. She hurried to Teya's side and stroked the girl's unruly auburn hair.

'Are you alright?'

'Don't.' Teya pushed the touch aside, giving a glimpse of haggard shadows haunting her expression.

Ying looked to Dallan. 'Did you…did it go…where's Perrin?'

He scrubbed at his jaw. 'I made it as far as the cells beneath the tower. He's there, alright. I almost had them convinced to release him to me. Then the weishi got a message and the boy was taken from the cells and upstairs in the Chinshi somewhere. No way I could stop them.'

A strangled cry burst from Teya and she covered her face.

Dallan groaned and rested his head on the chairback. 'Never mind. I know it was too much to ask of you. I'm sorry. Killing someone is harder than people think. The first few times, anyway.' He uttered a harsh laugh. 'It does get easier, unfortunately.'

Ying sent him a reproachful glare and he tried to shunt aside the burn of angry disappointment low in his guts. How the diyu was he supposed to get close to Han before the hunli ceremony made him too powerful to ever stop?

He was a fool for putting so much hope in such a slight chance. Teya was untried and inexperienced. For all her superficial streetwise bravado, she was still very young.

He rose and paced the room as he tried to think his way through the mess. It had all happened too fast. Han held every strong piece on the qi board. Dallan, and the eight juns he'd managed to convince to help, had few resources and little support. Most other juns were either complacent, or terrified of Han. Now that the man was on the brink of controlling the First and both Second jundoms, those few juns brave enough to stand against him would withdraw if decisive action wasn't taken soon.

Neri appeared in the doorway. 'There's no news from the Messenger House criers and no bells have rung from the Chinshi to alert the city to any deaths.' Her eyes glittered. 'I take it you failed?'

p136

Teya shoved up from the chair, rigid. 'Yes! I failed, alright. I got scared. His shangwei was there with a gouri sword at my throat!'

Dallan paused in his pacing. 'What? Why? Did he suspect you?'

She flushed pink and turned to the window. Outside, an early winter storm lowered dark clouds over the city. Lightning flickered and thunder growled in the distance, but Dallan suspected she saw none of it.

'No,' she murmured. 'I...I think he's suspicious of everyone. But I froze and missed my chance.' She glared. 'But you failed, too. You *promised* you'd get Perrin out.'

He groaned. 'I know. I'm...sorry. Gaisi!' He scrubbed at his head. 'Are you willing to try again?'

'Enough, Dallan,' Neri said, her voice hard. 'I can't support this anymore. I have a family and not enough power to stand against Han. We've run out of time. He and Jenna will be bound in the hunli ceremony tomorrow and there's nothing you can do.'

Dallan tried to ignore the sinking feeling in his stomach. She was his staunchest ally. If she felt this way, then no other juns would support him, either.

'Are you really prepared to let that...wisix hundan legalise slavery?' He pointed in the Chinshi's direction. 'Gaisi, Neri. You haven't *seen* what I have. You haven't seen how the slavemasters in Chengdu treat people...like animals.'

'No.' Her gaze softened. 'And I know you have a personal stake in this.'

He stilled.

She continued, 'I had people check into your background a little deeper. I know what that Melcor raiding party did to your family four years ago.' She glided into the room and touched Dallan's arm.

He barely resisted thrusting her away and held himself stiff beneath her touch. At the window, Teya turned, her eyes wide.

'Yes,' he replied evenly, suppressing a flare of old grief. 'It's true they took my daughter in a raid. I went after her…' He ground his teeth. 'I got her out but she died in my arms on the trip home. She was twelve.'

Neri touched his cheek and this time he did jerk away with an oath.

He strode to the cold fireplace and examined the small steel statue on the mantle. A model of the first ship full of colonists seeking freedom from oppression and war. He glared at Neri.

'And if you think the same sort of thing won't happen to you because your estate is a long way from the northern border with Melcor, then you're deluding yourself.'

He jabbed a finger at her. 'You really think you can introduce a slave-based economy to Mamlakah after five hundred years of freedom and have your people be unaffected? Untouched by the misery that comes with using other humans as forced labour? Not even a high-and-mighty funding-family jun can be that naïve and that entitled? Are you willing to throw away everything our ancestors came here for?' He brandished the statue at her then set it down with a snap.

Neri's jaw muscles worked. 'What I think, is that you've overstepped the line, Dallan. We are done.' A rumble of thunder cracked close overhead and rain slashed at the window. 'You may stay this night.' She surveyed the luxurious room, stopping at the wide window. 'But not here on the ground floor. Barrod will take you to the third floor guest room and keep watch at the door.'

'But—'

She cut off Dallan's protest with a cold glare. 'And you will go in the morning. I'll be returning to my estates the day after Han and Jenna's hunli ceremony celebrations. Assuming Han doesn't kill me for helping you.'

Ying whimpered.

Neri looked down her nose. 'Luckily, today I was able to buy something I know Han has always coveted: a mated pair of snow-serpents from Jadid.' She gave a scornful grunt. 'And I'll be pleading my case after the consummation hour is done. When Han and Jenna hear cases in the great hall.'

'Hedging your bets, were you?' Dallan sneered.

'Ying.' She ignored him. 'You'll go to Madina the morning and you…' she raked Teya with cool hauteur '…will go with her. Not that you deserve the privilege of such a position, but we can't have an untrained xintou running about.'

'I won't,' Teya spat.

'Then you can return to the streets.'

'Neri!' Dallan had to speak out. 'You can't send her away. If Han legalises slavery the people in the Migongs will be the first ones—'

'Silence!' Neri swept to the door. 'I will be in my chambers, packing. I don't wish to see any of you before you leave in the morning. I'll have your dinner sent to your new room. A servant will make a spare bed on the couch for you, Dallan, and Baddon will be stationed outside. Goodbye.'

She sent one last scathing glare over her shoulder. 'Dallan, I'm disappointed in you. Just be glad I'm not handing you over to Han.'

Dallan clenched his teeth, not trusting himself not to make things worse. The white rage in his soul burned too hot. He resisted the urge to throw the gouri colony-ship statue at her.

'Shunu Neri?' Ying ran to her Jun's side. 'Please don't send me back to Madina?' She tilted her head. 'The hunli ceremony will be ever so grand and beautiful. I've always, always wanted to go to the Jun First's hunli.' She cradled Neri's palm to her cheek, her lower lip sticking out. 'Please take me with you? I promise to be quiet and good and do *anything* you say.'

The hard angles of Neri's jaw eased. 'You are a good child, Ying. I'm sorry I dragged you into this. I do know it's not your fault.' She patted Ying's cheek. 'Very well. If you promise to be good, you can come. We leave for the opening ceremonies at dawn.' She frowned. 'Would you prefer to stay in this room for the night? I'm afraid Teya may not be a good influence on you.'

Ying cast her eyes down. 'Oh, no, shunu. I might be able to convince her to come to Xintou House, so I should stay with her.'

With a nod, Neri left the room.

A Future, Forged p141

CHAPTER TWENTY-ONE

TEYA

Barrod and three weishi ushered them wordlessly to the third floor. Teya followed Dallan and Ying, her stomach roiling as she tried to work out what to do. There was no escape. She had no choice, now. Not if she wanted Perrin home alive. Dallan had let her down. She had let them both down.

She choked on a groan, her chest tight.

The weishi let them into a much smaller room that smelled faintly of mould. No pictures or decorations softened the straight edges. Covers were still draped over some chairs, dust hung in the air from where the rest had been hastily stripped off by Neri's servants. The fireplace lay cold and unlit; the bed unmade, linens dumped on the faded grey quilt.

One window overlooked the back courtyard. Teya yanked aside threadbare curtains and peered out. If her arm was uninjured, she could climb the rough sandstone blocks. But not in her current state. And what good would that do, anyway?

She wrapped her arms around herself, shivering. The door clicked shut behind Baddor and his heavy footsteps stopped outside. His shadow cast an ominous darkness across the gap beneath. Teya checked on Dallan to see how he was taking the Jun's rejection.

He sank into a chair, swearing. Dust puffed around him.

Ying sat, staring at the door. 'I…I can't believe she did that. I don't understand.'

'I don't understand why you begged her to let you go to the ceremony,' Teya snarled. 'Typical xintou. Just looking out for yourself.' It shouldn't hurt or surprise her, but it did.

'That's not *fair*.' Ying glowered. 'I did it so I can be there, tomorrow, for you. Otherwise she would have sent me away with the first caravan to Madina and I'd never know what happened to you. I couldn't *bear* it.'

Speechless, Teya gaped at the girl. She'd given up the chance to get to safety? Why?

'What I don't understand,' Ying said to Dallan, 'is why she gave up on you like that, shenshi?'

Dallan's smile turned weary. 'Didn't you hear her? She has family.' His eyes narrowed. 'My weishi said she received a message from the Chinshi while we were out.'

Teya stifled a groan, knowing what must come next.

He nodded. 'It's no secret I'm staying here. I'm guessing Han threatened her children.' His mouth twisted. 'He would do the same to me if he could find my hunlinna and son. But I took them somewhere safe before I came.' The weight of sorrow and regret dragged at his expression, adding years. 'But I handled that badly by alienating Neri.'

'I didn't know about your daughter,' Ying said, tears pooling on her lids. 'I'm sorry.'

Teya said nothing, a band tightening around her voice.

Dallan waved Ying's sympathy away. 'What about you? I'm a first-family rebel with no support. You're risking your whole future if you keep helping me.'

'Keep helping?' Teya said. 'You're not going to stop?' Heat rushed to her cheeks. Why the diyu wouldn't the man quit? If he left Asalam now then surely Han wouldn't insist on his death? Then she could find her own way to get Perrin out, even if it took a little longer.

Dallan's expression darkened. 'I lost one child to slavers. I don't want anyone in Mamlakah to go through what I went through.' He swore. 'And, believe me, we don't want Han Gray-Saud on the First's throne. He is…broken.'

'What does that mean?' Ying asked.

'He's…he likes to have power over people,' he said, bitterness roughening his words. 'Enjoys making them do things they hate. Manipulating. Coercing. Bribing. Blackmailing. He likes playing with people's heads. His father was the same.'

Teya looked away.

'But why does Mistress Shana let him do it?' Ying wailed. 'She's Xintou. She's supposed to make sure her Bonded Jun is *good*. And why would anyone do such awful things to other people? I can't believe she knows about this.'

'Because he's out for himself,' Dallan said. 'All he's ever cared about is his needs and his desires. He's capable of recognising other people's needs. He has to be in order to manipulate them so well. But his always come first in the long run.'

'And Shana is the same,' Teya said. 'She…I heard her offer to break someone's wards. Said they would do anything he liked when she was finished.'

'Gouri,' Dallan muttered.

'We have to stop him. I'll help,' Ying said. 'But I'm not sure what I can do, now. With Mistress Rua away and Jenna's Xintou sick, there's no-one to stop Shenshi Han and Mistress Shana, even if I sent a message to Xintou House in Madina and told the Mistresses what was happening. Besides, I'm only thirteen. They probably wouldn't believe me, anyway.'

Both of them turned to Teya and she shrank further into the corner. A knock on the door interrupted. Relief frissoned through her stomach. A servant entered bearing a tray holding three bowls of miso soup and a half-loaf of crusty dark bread. Another arrived carrying plates and more food.

They hurried away and the lock clicked shut.

Dallan gave a wry laugh. 'At least she's not starving us, even if we are prisoners for the night.' He gestured. 'Eat, you two. I'll be back in a minute.' He disappeared into the bathroom.

Ying fussed over cutlery and place settings on the low table. Teya touched the phial in her pocket.

It would be so easy.

She quashed a flutter in her belly and sauntered over to the table. What choice did she have, now?

p146

'Let me help.' She picked up a bowl of soup, passing one hand deftly over the top as she slid it into place before the chair Dallan had last occupied. Then she sat at the opposite end of the tiny table, her knees weak and heart racing.

She patted the seat next to her. 'Sit here, Ying. At least we'll have one last evening together.' Hopefully the words didn't sound as stilted as they felt.

A sunny smile lit Ying's round face. 'But you will come with me to Xintou House, won't you? After the ceremony tomorrow? I'm sure we can work out some way to help Perrin. And you heard Shenshi Johnston. He won't quit.'

Teya uttered a non-committal grunt. She spooned a mouthful of the richly-flavoured, salty soup and swallowed though it tasted sourly of guilt and betrayal.

Dallan returned, sat, and gathered his spoon.

Teya watched him from beneath her lashes, no longer tasting the food even as it scalded her palate.

He dipped the spoon twice and let the yellowish liquid dribble into the bowl. 'I'm not particularly hungry.'

Teya fought the urge to yell at him. Or to throw up. Her own hunger vanished and she stared blankly at the food. Perrin. This was the only way to save him. The thought of her cheeky, indomitable brother enslaved—used by Han—was enough. Had to be enough.

'You should eat, shenshi,' she said, sipping again at her broth. 'Then we can plan what to do next to stop Han.'

'You'll still help? I know it's a long shot, Tey.' He smiled understandingly. 'And I know you're scared for Perrin. I'm afraid for him, too. And for my own son. And the children in the Migongs and other poor areas. They're all at risk if Han succeeds in this. But with your gift and a little luck, I think we can do it.'

He dipped his spoon and lifted it.

'Don't!' Teya smacked the utensil from his hand and threw the bowl onto the floor. The delicate grey and white ceramic shattered into three pieces and sprayed hot soup and bits of tofu and vegetable across the timber. She stood over the table, shaking, snatching for air that seemed too thin.

CHAPTER TWENTY-TWO

TEYA

Dallan stared at Teya, his mouth still open. She waited for him to strike her, to yell, to call for Barrod.

'What made you change your mind?' he finally said, brushing soup off his skin.

She collapsed onto her chair. 'You knew?'

'Suspected.'

'I don't understand!' Ying complained.

Teya produced the blue phial and set it on the table. It fell over and rolled toward the edge.

Dallan snatched it and sniffed at the opening. 'Gu-spider venom? Yes, poisoning is very much Han's style.'

Ying whimpered and shoved her soup away.

He studied the broken bowl and the liquid spread across the floor. 'He found out about Perrin and who you are, I assume?' He placed the phial on the table.

Teya nodded, unable to speak. What had she done? Had she just condemned her brother to a life of unspeakable torment?

'Han offered to free Perrin if you killed me,' Dallan said. 'Tell me?'

'I wasn't ready,' Teya whispered. 'When I got to his room I panicked because his shangwei was there and I thought he must recognise me from last night. So I didn't get an illusion ready fast enough. Then I lost the chance to break Han's wards because I…couldn't think straight.' She shivered. 'I don't know what was wrong with me! Why couldn't I do it?'

'It's ok,' Dallan said. 'It's normal to be flustered and make mistakes under that sort of pressure. If we'd had time to practice…' He waved that aside. 'Nevermind. Keep going.'

She steadied herself and repeated everything Han had said and done, including her mother's appearance and the Xintou, Shana's involvement.

'He took your dagger. And now…' she trailed off, indicating the broken bowl. 'Now he'll do horrible things to Perrin and it's my fault!' She held tears in by sheer force of will. She would *not* cry. Only children cried.

Ying's plump arms went around her. The girl buried her face in Teya's neck and cried for her, warm tears sliding down Teya's cold skin.

Dallan shifted closer and stroked Teya's hair. 'Hey. It's alright. I'm a zift for putting you in such a position in the first place.' He smiled faintly. 'But thank you for not killing me.'

She chewed her lip, still uncertain she'd made the right choice. 'But what do we do, now? If you're not dead, how will I get Perrin? We have no-one to help and one day to stop Han.'

He sat back. 'Actually, you may have given me a good idea. Han did say he wanted to hear the Messenger House runners cry my death over the city, right?'
p150

Teya groaned. 'Please tell me you're not going to pretend to be a dead body and somehow use that to get into the Chinshi. Because he's not that stupid.'

Laughing, Dallan shook his head. 'There would be no reason for the body of a Johnston to be taken to the Chinshi. I'd be shipped to my estates and that's no help. But let's give him the satisfaction of hearing I'm dead.'

'How will that help? You can't go into hiding forever.'

He scratched at the two-day growth on his jaw. 'No. But once Han thinks I'm dead he may not be so cautious. We'll find a way in. And Ying will already be inside, in Neri's entourage.'

'Don't ask me to cast illusions,' Teya said miserably. 'I'd let you down again.'

He patted her wrist and took his seat again. 'You won't.'

'Can't we…' Ying rubbed at her cheeks and sniffed '…talk to the Law Mistresses? If we explain they'll get Perrin out.'

Dallan's expression hardened. 'Don't be naïve, Ying. Shana *is* the head Law Mistress here in Asalam. The other three in Asalam defer to her rulings. I assume, since they haven't reported her to Mistress Rua of Xintou House, either Han has something over them, or Shana does. Either way, they can't be trusted.'

Ying blanched. 'But they're *xintou.* How could so many of them betray *everything* the House stands for? It doesn't make sense! I don't believe it.'

Frowning, Dallan ran his hand over his hair. 'You could be right. I've never heard of so many xintou turning against their House at one time, in one city. What are Shana's gifts, do you know?'

Ying shook her head. 'But only the strongest xintou are Bonded to juns. She'll be telepathic. Probably have empathy and maybe the ability to broadcast her thoughts and feelings to many people at once—though that's rarer. I don't think she has foreseeing, or she would have seen Teya's coming today before it happened.'

'Good point.' Dallan paced the room. 'We need to plan and you...' he pointed at Teya '...need to practice getting through wards quickly.'

'Then what? How do we get close to Han?'

'Like I said, there might be another way in.'

Teya eyed him askance.

From within his jacket, he first produced her bronze dagger, then a folded piece of yellowed bamboo paper. He unfolded the paper, shifted the remains of their meals aside and laid it on the table.

'It's a plan of the Chinshi. I stole it from the archive vault, which is downstairs next to the prison cells. I'd seen it once before, years ago, so it was easy enough to find.'

Teya shot to her feet, glowering at him. 'So, you going for Perrin? Me going to kill Han? It was all...what...a lie and a distraction so you could get a *map*?'

'Calm down!' He towered over her. 'Stop thinking the worst of everyone. When they took Perrin I assumed *something* had gone wrong and finding the map was the only other option I had. If they'd captured you, then I needed this to get you both out.' He met her fierceness with honest intensity. 'I wasn't going to leave you there. Either of you. I don't renege on my promises.'

She examined him but there was no trace of a lie. For the first time she wished her xintou skills included telepathy; that she could read him. But she couldn't, and whether his words were true was yet to be seen. She returned to the table and pored over the map.

It took a while for the complex collection of lines and tiny words to make sense, then she understood. The building was separated into floors, each one drawn as an outline.

Down one side of the paper was a series of strange symbols. They represented stairs, doors, where wine was stored, the well in the kitchen courtyard. And the bath-house and stables complex behind the house proper—where water entered, pumped from the hot springs outside the city.

'Here.' Dallan pointed to part of the drawing. 'This is the prison cells under the south tower. And Jenna's quarters— where Han will be—are here. Higher up in the same tower.' He pointed to a large, rectangular space in a separate drawing.

'But we don't want to kill Jenna. And why would Han be—' Her cheeks warmed and she took in Ying's innocence. 'Oh.'

Ying giggled. 'I'm not ignorant. I know what you're talking about.'

Teya looked sidelong at Dallan. 'You don't mean it? You want me to try and kill Han *in* the bedroom, with his new hunlinna right there? During the consummation hour?'

He chuckled. 'Can you think of a time or place when he will be less guarded and less wary? Especially if he thinks I'm dead. And Jenna has no fighting skills. She won't be able to stop you.'

'But what if Perrin isn't in the prison cells any more?'

'Once Han hears the news of my death, he should release Perrin.'

'He won't.' She folded her arms, grimacing when the injured shoulder reminded her it was far from healed.

'Why would he keep Perrin? He can't ransom the boy for money. While I admit he's a wisix hundan, there's no benefit in breaking his promise to you.'

Teya pretended deep interest in the map. 'I don't trust him, that's all.'

Dallan observed her closely. 'Is there some other reason, Teya? Is Perrin…' he frowned '…a male xintou?'

She stilled. 'He's never done anything like what I can do. Why?'

'Xintou abilities don't show until puberty, anyway,' Ying put in. 'But male xintou are really rare. And…' her voice dropped to a whisper '…really dangerous. But no-one remembers why.'

'That's what worries me.' Dallan's scowl deepened. 'I thought that might be why Han wanted him, if you're so sure he will.'

p154

'Oh, he will. Like you said: he likes to control people and he won't be happy that Perrin and I escaped the first time.' Hoping to change the subject, Teya bent over the map's confusing welter of lines, circles and cramped writing in faded ink. 'And what do we do about Shana?'

'First things first. Let's get Perrin, then my dagger, then we kill Han.'

She picked up her own bronze dagger and tucked it into her belt. Then she regarded him. 'Why is it so important to use that dagger? And don't give me that feihua about alzin armour. When he took it he said something about you wanting it to be the weapon that killed him.' When he didn't reply, only pensively studied the map, she folded her arms again. 'I'm not helping if you don't tell me.'

He sank into his chair with a weary sigh. 'When I first went to Asalam Weishi House I was twelve or so. Han was fourteen. Charismatic. Rich. Handsome.' Wintry self-disdain chilled his expression. 'I was flattered when he sought me out. Groomed me. When I turned sixteen we were lovers for a few months.' His jaw hardened. 'Until a new student transferred from Madina Weishi House and I saw what Han really was.'

'What happened?'

He lifted his eyes and they harboured such bleakness Teya flinched. 'He likes to twist people's thinking. To manipulate them. To use and discard them. He tried to do it to me. But I'd grown up with a jun for a friend and a xintou for a teacher, so I understood mindgames. But Han drove the new lad to suicide. The boy had become a good friend of mine. If Han did it out of jealousy or spite, I don't know.'

His jaw worked. 'I found the body. And the note. When I reported him to the House Master, Han used his influence to save his own neck and lay the blame on me. I quit to save my parents' grief. If I hadn't, Han would have had me kicked out of the House.'

He half-drew his sword and ran a thumb over the dull white yanstone embedded in the pommel. 'Four more boys took their own lives in the two years he stayed after I left. He knows why I want to put my dagger into him.'

Teya thrust guilt aside. She should have killed him today. 'What do I do?'

He squeezed her wrist. 'Thank you. When it's all over, I'll make sure you and Perrin are safe and well cared-for.'

She snorted. 'You make it sound easy.'

'Not easy,' he replied, wryly. 'But I can't afford to give in to pessimism. You're my best hope of saving this jundom. I'm counting on you. And you can count on me.'

Ying wormed her way under Teya's arm. 'And me.'

Uneasy, Teya broke free and wandered over to the now-dark window. Outside the thunderstorm still growled and flashed, silhouetting the Chinshi's twin towers against brilliant flares of purple-white light. Soft golden lamps glowed in windows all over the city. Shadows of people passed before them, dancing, walking, running; living ordinary lives unaffected by the tide of change about to swamp them.

A tide she was supposed to hold back and not drown in. As much as they might say she could count on them, neither Ying nor Dallan could take her place in this madness.

'Right.' She turned. 'We'd best practice my illusion-casting and plan how we're going to convince Neri you're dead, then.'

Ying sent her a dubious look. 'You'll need to stop being angry if you want to be strong enough to break Han Gray-Saud's wards.'

With a bitter laugh, Teya rolled her eyes. 'That's like asking the hot springs to stop being hot.'

'But you don't understand—'

'Leave it, Ying! You're not my mother. I'm fine the way I am. Anger at Gray-Saud helped me survive these last five years. There's no way I can start being all loving toward him. You don't know what he did.'

'I don't mean—'

Teya cut her off with a glare and addressed Dallan. 'What do I do and how do I get into the Chinshi?'

'You'll go in the front door again, secure Perrin's release and hand him to Ying in the main hall. Then she—'

'I can't go in the front. If Han sees me again, he'll keep me and Perrin, both,' she said.

'You don't know—'

She regarded him coldly.

He nodded. 'Very well. So how do we get you and I in, then? Because I'll be dead so I can't walk in the front door, either.'

She peered at the map, again.

'What about this?' She pointed. 'You can't fit, but I can. And I think I know another way for you to get inside.'

CHAPTER TWENTY-THREE

Ying screamed just after dawn.

Teya peeked through a gap in the clothes closet door. Barrod burst into the room, weapon drawn. Ying, standing by the bed, pointed at Dallan's body, sprawled in the middle of the floor.

Teya focussed on Barrod's wards, ensuring the illusion was strong and steady. The weishi blanched and knelt by Dallan. Teya could see the rise and fall of Dallan's chest, but to Barrod it ought to look like the man lay still and lifeless, with a pool of blood soaking his shirt and puddling under his body.

Neri appeared in the doorway, already resplendent in a deep grey robe with intricate copper embroidery around the neck and cuffs. Teya drove the illusion through her wards, glad now she had spent hours training with Ying last night. A wave of weakness swept through her, but she held herself strong. She should have eaten something.

Neri paled and sagged against the doorframe.

Barrod swore. 'What happened?'

Ying shrank. 'W-when I woke, he was dead and Teya was gone.'

Barrod scanned the room. The window stood open, the heavy velvet curtains swaying in the dawn breeze. He ran over and thrust his head outside. Teya inserted a carefully-constructed image of herself, fleeing from the house's courtyard. Hopefully he wouldn't question her ability to scale the wall, injured as she was.

Neri approached the body, one trembling hand over her mouth. Teya set her jaw. Holding two illusions at once was difficult.

Spinning on his heel, Barrod rushed out the door, yelling. His footsteps clattered on the stairs and more voices echoed in the depths of the house. Teya let his mind go. Now he could chase shadows without her input. She centred on Neri.

The jun knelt at Dallan's side and shakily touched his jugular. Teya blocked the awareness of sensory input with an illusion of cold skin and no pulse. After a long silence, Neri rose, her shoulders slumped and face haggard.

She reached out to Ying. 'I'm sorry, child. He's dead. Oh, I'm a fool for accepting that girl. I knew she was trouble the second I saw her.' She considered Dallan bleakly. 'And we have no time to mourn him for we must get ready and leave for the ceremonies. I can't afford to get on Han's bad side.'

Ying's lower lip trembled. 'But why would Teya do this?'

In the closet's darkness, Teya smiled. The kid was a pretty good actor.

p160

'I suppose Han offered her brother's life in exchange for Dallan's and she found it too hard to resist.' Neri gazed one last time at the body and turned away, her throat working. 'He was a good man. Naïve in his belief in the best in people, but a good man. I wish…' She shook her head. 'Nevermind. Let's go.'

With a glance at the cupboard, Ying gathered her belongings and trailed Neri out the door. The lock clicked shut behind them.

Teya emerged from the cupboard. Dallan rolled to his feet and joined her at the door.

'Naïve!' He snorted. Teya put a finger to her lips.

He whispered, 'Now we need to get into the storehouse where Neri has those snow-serpents caged. Think you can project the image of that servant, who brought dinner, carrying my body if we meet anyone?'

Teya nodded.

'Here.' He draped his tartan cloak—reversed to show the black lining—over her shoulders. 'It's cold out. Once I'm inside the Chinshi walls, you go to the entry point. When you're inside, wait for me at the exit point. It should be empty.'

His brow clouded. He hauled her into a rough hug and kissed her forehead. 'Be safe, alright?'

'I know,' she said, trying to ignore the pang of longing in her chest. 'You need me.'

He held her away. 'Actually, I'm looking forward to introducing you and Perrin to my hunlinna and son. They'll like you.' He hesitated and added, 'When this is over, if your mother is amenable, the village near my estates could use a good midwife. There's a place for you all, if you want.'

Turning away, he produced two slender, steel lockpicks from a compartment in the heel of his boot, and released the doorlock. Then he crept out and, after a moment, Teya followed, her heart stuttering.

CHAPTER TWENTY-FOUR

TEYA

Teya wrapped Dallan's cloak closer about herself and tucked her hands under her armpits as she waited in the crowd along the causeway leading to the Chinshi's front façade. A parade of juns and rich merchants, who'd been invited to the hunli ceremony, sauntered and rode between a cheering crowd of common folk.

She'd been waiting for an hour, now.

The sun played hide and seek behind thick, dark clouds. Occasional flurries of fine, cold rain made the ground slick but didn't dampen the party atmosphere.

She studied the crowd milling about in the huge courtyard before the Chinshi. Thousands of people had arrived to wait for the bells that would announce the end of the Jun First's hunli ceremony. Women were brilliant flowers, dressed in silks and bright cloths; many wearing the half-veil favoured by those of higher caste. Men, in more sober robes, drank jiu and wine from wineseller stands dotted around the courtyard.

Families showed their loyalty to their ranking jun by wearing a scarf or ribbon of the jun's colours. Everywhere fluttered scraps of black and silver, black and copper, black and gold. Most of those present were allied to Han or the Jun First, by the looks of it. With a smattering of purples and greens to for the two Jun Second jundoms.

Weaving between the chattering people were entertainers of all descriptions: dancers in gauzy veils, musicians twanging ouds, playing pipes, or tapping drums; enterprising merchants selling hastily-made gew-gaws to commemorate the hunli; others carrying trays of steaming pork buns and dumplings.

The rich, meaty scents made Teya's stomach rumble, for Dallan's 'death' this morning had made her miss breakfast. She could almost hear Ying's mothering demands that she eat something.

She waited until a bun-vendor wandered past, faded herself, and stole two buns and two dumplings, almost burning her tongue when she ate them in haste. She stole a cup of redberry juice to wash them down and wiped away the scarlet liquid. She would have enough energy now, hopefully.

Amongst the chatter, music and laughter, the Messenger House criers announcing Dallan Johnston's death went almost unheard. Hard-faced city junren in Han's colours followed close on the criers' heels, observing people and taking the names of anyone who seemed upset at the news.

The food churned in her stomach and she removed herself from the junrens' line of sight.

The braying of brass trumpets announced the arrival of the next jun. Teya craned to see through the mass of heads. There. Neri reclined in a palanquin, her eyes veiled by thin copper-coloured silk, nodding regally to the crowds of cheering people as she passed. Seated opposite, bolt upright, was Ying. The gleaming gold silk robes and veil of a xintou seemed heavy and thick on her small shoulders.

Teya directed her attention to Neri's entourage. A pair of black-and-white striped che-ma were harnessed to a huge cage on wooden wheels. The che-mas' eyes rolled and they whickered and shook their stiff manes. They strained at the harness and pulled the cage along jerkily, their hooves clattering on the stone road. Their fear was understandable. The cage held a pair of huge, white-furred snow-serpents.

Teya stared in awe. She'd heard of the black-and-blue quetzal serpents from the warmer northern jundoms, and seen a green-furred one from the Makaan desert, northeast of Madina. But the snow-serpents from Jadid were mountain-dwelling and rarely caught.

They twined and coiled around each other in the close-barred cage. Their heads were larger than Teya's. Their fangs longer than her forearm. Their white-blue eyes glittered, cold and soullessly frightening.

A mated pair would make Han the envy of all other juns. Which was precisely his aim.

He always wanted what he couldn't have. Now, as consort to the Jun First, he could have anything. What would he do with that power?

Teya squinted as sunlight flared through a gap in the clouds.

The cage's base was skirted with a fall of copper and grey silk which hid the gap beneath. Dallan lay hidden beneath the cage, holding tight to the undercarriage. With her injured arm, she wouldn't have had the strength to hold on. No way of telling, though, if he had made it this far.

Would he be there when she emerged into the Chinshi's interior, later? She set her jaw. Even if he wasn't, she had to try and free Perrin. No point in asking Han for her brother's release. Even before Dallan's stories of how Han behaved in Weishi House, she'd known it was hopeless.

He would never let her, or Perrin, go. Not alive, anyway.

Neri's group passed out of view and the Chinshi's great timber gates creaked closed on the last of the officially-invited guests. Outside, the people of Asalam prepared to celebrate the binding of their Jun First.

Dragon dancers sprang into action, leaping from roof to roof around the courtyard. The great red dragon flapped its mouth and rolled its eyes, the sinuous body undulating behind on human legs. A spray of rare and expensive fireworks gushed into the peridot sky in a flare of red sparkles. A cheer erupted from the throng. The pleasantly-acrid smoke from the fireworks settled on the crowd, mingling with hints of blackweed, rain, and roasting meats.

Teya slipped away.

She worked her way around the Chinshi via the back streets. Even there people were dancing and drinking jiu. Parties in the larger houses vomited guests and entertainers out into the street. It seemed like the entire town was taking the day off, for she encountered few carts or merchants laden with goods and most shops were closed.

But the city junren, in Han's colours, were out in force. Three times she was obliged to hide and once she had to flip over a fence and crouch behind it until the pair of guards passed. A sharp pain reminded her of the injury and she prodded her shoulder. No blood, but the wound was hot and painful. She flexed her fingers, dismayed to find them swollen and weak.

When she found the entry point outside the Chinshi's west wall, her luck was in. There were no people or junren around. The manhole was tucked away in an alley between the rambling buildings of Weishi House, and a herbalist's shop.

Teya paused outside the window. Could she buy more poison and feed it to Han, somehow? No. She had no coin and, since he had trained in Weishi House, he would know about poisons and how to cure them. He might even have food tasters.

She found the manhole at the alley's end and kicked aside a layer of rubbish and leaves that obscured it. Then she examined it for a long time, debating. The conduit fed hot water from the springs high on the cliffs, west of the city.

Could she do this? Normally she was a strong swimmer, but with an injured shoulder... And she would need to hold her breath. Let the current carry her a hundred metres from this point. Under the Chinshi's solid stone walls, to the bath house.

She shuddered. For Perrin. She could do this for him.

Teya levered the manhole and slid it aside, hissing at the strain in her arm. Steam roiled from the darkness and the rush of water burbled and flicked droplets out on to the road. The space was barely large enough to fit her shoulders. She folded Dallan's cloak and hid it behind a stack of timber to one side then returned to regard the dark water.

Dallan had assured her there would be light from the side conduits leading to houses. It was, apparently, a rite of passage in Weishi House to make this run from the House all the way beneath the Chinshi and out the other side. More than three hundred metres.

Surely she could make a hundred. Teya stared at the water and gulped air.

Dallan had given her precise instructions. The second conduit to the left would access the Chinshi bath house. There would be a handle to grab, put there for the maintenance children.

But they had air tubes.

No. She could do this. The current would be fast enough to carry her there before she ran out of breath.

She could do this.

She could.

The steady thump of marching feet from the main street gave her impetus. Junren. At least half a dozen, by the sounds of it; swordbelts jingling, the leader shouting orders to her men. Closer with every step. No more time to think about it.

Teya climbed into the hole and stood on the tunnel's brick-lined floor, her head above the street. She painfully dragged the manhole cover closer, struggling one-armed with the heavy timber slab.

The stomp of feet drew closer. A few more metres and they would be at the alley's entry, able to see her.

Ignoring the pain, she used both hands and hauled the lid on. She dragged three deep breaths, filling her lungs right to the bottom each time.

On the fourth she crouched and dropped the lid into place. Only a fingerswidth of air remained between the water's surface and the cover's underside.

All was darkness and womb-like warmth around her. The current tugged at her legs.

She gripped the tunnel's upper edge at her hip height.

Before she could panic, she lifted her feet and sank into the flow of water.

CHAPTER TWENTY-FIVE

DALLAN

Dallan held on until his arms and legs burned and he could no longer hold his place beneath the cart. Only then did he let go and lower himself to the damp cobblestones. He lay there, massaging blood into his hands and waiting for his muscles to stop trembling.

The snow-serpent cart had trundled the dozen or so blocks from Neri's house to the Chinshi at a pace that made Dallan want to scream with frustration. When it finally reached the Jun First's Asalam residence, it had sat in the middle of the courtyard inside the walls forever, surrounded by hurrying people on all sides. Then, at last, someone had directed a servant to take it behind the house to the stables.

Dallan had almost cried out in relief when the che-ma were unhitched and the cart dragged off to one side. Even then it had taken far too long for the stableyard to empty of servants and ostlers.

Now, he peered out from beneath the silk curtain. No-one. He held his scabbard off the ground and scrambled from beneath the cart. The two big snakes inside hissed at him, baring fangs longer than his hand. One struck at the bars, the sound of its snout hitting metal ringing out in the empty courtyard. He leapt aside with an oath, his heart skipping.

Brushing dirt off his clothes, he oriented himself. First, to find out if Perrin was in the prison cells. If the map was right, a second entrance existed through the kitchens.

He surveyed the rear of the house—little more than a large, square block, studded with windows. Behind him lay the stables, servants' quarters, and the kitchen garden and orchard that provided for the house.

The map showed the ground floor rear was mostly kitchen, storage. Hard against the northern wall stood the huge bath house that catered to the whole household. The Jun First had her own bath room upstairs, in her chambers.

The bath house would be where Teya came out. With any luck, all the servants would be too busy to bathe at this time and it would be empty. And would have towels and probably spare clothes for her to steal.

A stone-lined well protruded from the ground not far from the kitchen door. The house had piped water, so the well must be for use by the stablehands for watering animals and cleaning. He hurried over and peered in. Only water rippled in the bottom, black and silver and hazed in steam. A safe place for Teya to emerge if she missed the exit for the bath house. Greenish-bronze handholds formed a ladder up the slimy walls.

For now, he needed to get inside and see if Perrin was in the prison cells. No time to try and find a servant's livery. Hopefully his own, expensive, dark blue-and-green tunic and trous would allow him to pass as a lost guest and he could bluff his way in if seen.

He scanned the sun, hazed behind the tattered remnants of rainclouds. Maybe half an hour to midday. Once the hunli ceremony was complete, the house bells would toll, along with all those around town.

According to tradition, Han and Jenna would withdraw for an hour to their chambers to consummate the bond. Then they would reappear to host the feast and hear special pleas from the juns.

That hour was the window for success. But there were so many 'ifs'. So many variables.

Not the least of which was Teya, herself. Would she follow through? Would she make her way to the bedroom and trust him to do his part in releasing Perrin while she did hers? She clearly had little respect for any juns or friends of juns. Was he mad to put all his hope into the hands of a girl who wanted nothing to do with him?

How else could he possibly get close to Han? He couldn't. Han was too wary.

But, perhaps, he could check and make sure she kept her end of the bargain—at least as far as arriving in the bath house.

Which meant he had to find the prison cells, fast. If, as Teya suspected, Han had kept Perrin close by after meeting Teya, the trip would be a waste of time. But he'd promised.

Why she thought the boy would be so important to Han was a mystery. Was there something special about the child that Han knew? Could the earlier hypothesis—that the boy was a male xintou—be right?

If it were… If the vague rumours about the extraordinary power of a male xintou were true, then a tool like that in Han's control… The psychological manipulation Han could wield on a boy so young and impressionable… Dallan shuddered. The weapon Han would create…that was a terrifying thought.

Dallan scratched at his chin. Had Teya told the truth about the boy when he'd asked? She had seemed uncomfortable at the time but he'd put it down to her intention of killing him on Han's command. And, as Ying said, the boy's powers wouldn't show until puberty, so Teya wouldn't know if her brother was xintou, anyway.

He shook himself. Nothing to be done about it now. He needed to get them all safely through this mess.

He stopped with one hand on the kitchen door handle, listening. Inside a din of raised voices and the clanking of metal attested to a kitchen overwhelmed by the day's demands. He cracked the door and slipped inside.

The smell of roasting lu-deer mingled with the salty odour of dumplings and the sweetness of something with redberries teased him. His mouth watered and his stomach rumbled, reminding him of a dinner and breakfast missed.

The massive kitchen was brightly-lit with electric bulbs, clouded by smoke and steam high above. Three huge brick ovens were set in the northern wall, their heat shielded with what must be some sort of nickel-based heat-resistant alloy doors. No expense spared for the Jun First's country house.
p174

A red-faced, sweat-slicked woman wrenched a door open and used a long-handled implement to remove a loaf of bread. She transferred it to a bench and yelled a command at a harried-looking teenage boy who grabbed at the loaf. He snatched his hand away, howling.

Five people left their stations to cluster about the boy, offering advice, cold water and sympathy.

Dallan seized the moment. He edged around the wall, ducking to avoid copper pans hanging low, and aimed for a door set in the southern wall. On his way past a bench, he stole a slender boning knife to replace his lost dagger. As an afterthought, he speared a slab of roast lu-deer.

The door opened under his touch and he edged through unhindered. Once inside, he paused, shoved the meat into his mouth and swallowed in a hurry. Better than nothing and it tasted delicious.

A narrow stone hallway, dimlit with two bulbs, drove west inside the walls of the keep. He crept down a shallow flight of stairs and peered around the corner at the end.

He withdrew. Four guards. Two lounging by the main entrance that lead to the front of the house. Two at a table set close to the cellblock door. How the diyu was he supposed to get inside when Han must have warned his staff to watch out after last time?

He gripped the hilt of his steel sword, and the boning knife. He wasn't a bad fighter, but against four trained weishi? There had to be another way. If he met Teya in the bath house, she could cast an illusion, perhaps. Her practice with Ying had strengthened her gift a little. Surely she could trick three or four minds, now.

He turned to head for the kitchen.

A sword lay at his throat. He stilled and slowly raised his hands.

'I was thinking we'd see you here, Shenshi Johnston,' Gennar Gen-kin said, smiling. 'Didn't trust that girl to follow through.'

Dallan swore.

CHAPTER TWENTY-SIX

TEYA

The tunnel was darker than Teya had expected. The water faster, hotter and tasting of sulphur. Her eyes stung and she squinted, trying to make out shapes in the gloom.

She fought the urge to cry out. She splayed her hands and feet against the walls, trying to slow down and feel for exits.

A glimpse of watery green light flashed past on her left. And another.

Her fingers brushed a gap on the left. Was that one or two? Had she missed the exit?

Her lungs burned. She had to breathe soon. Her heart pounded, using precious oxygen. She tried to detach herself, to calm her thoughts, but panic surged like the water.

There. On the left, a hole. Brightly lit and large. That had to be it.

The dark silhouette of a handle. She snatched at it but her weakened right hand couldn't hold her weight. She flipped over and held tight with her left. Her legs dangled in the flow. Kicking hard, she hauled herself into the side tunnel and pushed for the light.

Close now. Dallan said this came out inside an open-topped holding tank.

Her vision blurred. She had to breathe.

No. She could do this.

Her outstretched hands hit something hard. A metal grill. Frantically, she felt it from side to side. It stretched across the tunnel's opening. Beyond and above she could see the shimmering water surface. Air and freedom lay there.

She reversed her position and braced against the tunnel walls.

Kick. The sound of her boots on metal reverberated through the water.

Kick. Nothing. No give. The mesh was secure.

Kick.

It had to work. She had to get out. Had to breathe.

Kick.

The tunnel darkened. Her chest ached.

Against her will, Teya opened her mouth.

#

TEYA

'Teya!'

Someone shouted her name from a long way off. Her bed was cold and hard. She was freezing, bone-deep, every muscle. She lay on her stomach. Her shoulder hurt. Someone shouted her name again. Said something else, too, but the words were muffled. Something heavy pounded on her chest. Why couldn't she breathe?

She coughed and water sprayed from her nose. Weight on her back again and more water bubbled from between her lips. She managed to gulp air and coughed out more water. Coughed until knives stabbed her chest and she could barely see through tears. Then she vomited yet more water onto the stone floor.

Someone helped her sit up and brushed sodden hair from her bleary eyes and water from her mouth.

Dallan's face swam into view. With a shaky hand, she touched the purpling bruise on his jaw.

'Wh…what happened?' she whispered, coughing again. The smell of piss and sweat registered and she gagged. Every breath hurt. 'Where are we?'

He sighed. 'In the prison cells under the Chinshi. We failed. I'm sorry, Tey. They caught both of us.' He glanced over his shoulder. 'And Perrin's not in here with us, either.'

Teya scrubbed snot and water from her cheeks and slumped against the thick bronze prison cell bars. Only then did the sheer number of people in the space register.

She curled into a ball, shivering. Her clothes were soaked, her strength gone. A spreading darkness stained the shirt red over her shoulder.

Dallan settled beside her, his arm warm against hers. 'What happened?'

She coughed again, dragging painful breaths. 'Metal grill over…the tunnel exit. I couldn't kick it in. Then I blacked out.' More coughing but at least breathing was getting easier.

'That's new. Gouri.' He groaned. 'I'm a complete shazi.'

'How did I get here?' She surveyed the other inmates. There was hardly enough room for everyone to sit and several stood, slumped against the walls, faces blank and hopeless. Most were teenagers or in their early twenties. Three children as young as five or six huddled together in one corner.

'Who are all these people?' she whispered.

'Mostly youngsters caught out after curfew. Waiting for their parents to pay ransom, if they can.' Dallan jerked a thumb over his shoulder. 'A bath house servant brought you in. Heard you making a noise and dragged you out. They're holding you here until the hunli and consummation hour are over. Then we'll both be brought before Han and Jenna.'

'Why me?'

'Because the weishi were going to send you to the slavers until I told them you were Helva Connor's daughter. They don't believe me, but they're not willing to take the chance I might be right.'

'Oh, gouri. What a mess. Ying?'

'Haven't been able to reach her. We agreed she would get in touch with me ten minutes after the bells rang. It's too early, so either she's not listening for me, or she's been removed from the hall and sent home. No way of knowing.'

Overhead, muffled by the thick stone walls, the house bells clamoured joyously. The hunli ceremony was over.

Han was consort to the Jun First.

How long would he wait before killing Jenna and taking the throne for himself? Teya buried her face in her hands.

A Future, Forged p181

CHAPTER TWENTY-SEVEN

DALLAN

Dallan cocked an ear. 'Now there's an hour before Han and Jenna receive people into the audience chamber and hear their pleas. And ours. Ten minutes before Ying contacts me.'

'What good will that do?' Teya muttered. 'She's a kid surrounded by adults. Neri won't let her out of her sight, now. And definitely won't listen to her.'

He rested his head on the bars. She was right. How the diyu had he gone so wrong? He'd been mad to think he could do this on his own, with only a fifteen-year-old girl for help. Overthrowing a tyrant needed the support of thousands of people and all the juns. One person—or even two—couldn't make a difference. Neri had been right. He was naïve.

He wiped at his face.

Beside him, Teya sat in gloomy silence, her attention fixed on her hands, clasped loosely in her lap.

'So,' she said, coughing again. 'In an hour Han is officially Jun First Consort. And Neri will plead for forgiveness for helping you. Will he give it?'

'I don't know,' Dallan admitted, his hopes sinking. Han was likely to make an example of Neri. To show the other juns what came of trying to work together against his rule.

Teya eyed him beneath her lashes. 'What about Ying? Will she be punished?'

'I don't know. If Shana suspects Ying knows she has turned against Xintou House, then I don't like Ying's chances.'

'And Perrin?' Her throat worked. 'What will he do to Perrin?'

'Gouri!' Dallan stood, holding the bars so tight his fingertips numbed. 'I don't know, alright? What's so important about Perrin, anyway? Why would Han care about him? Did you lie to me? Is he a male xintou?'

She paled and lowered her eyes. 'No, of course not!'

'Then what? Why would Han keep him once he thought I was dead? Why did you believe he wouldn't release the boy after you fulfilled your part of the bargain and killed me?'

But she turned away and said nothing.

Dallan leaned on his forearm and stared through the bars at freedom. 'I tried, Teya. I tried to get the juns to work together and stop this. I failed.' He swore.

He would never see his hunlinna and son again. There would be no-one to protect them from Gray-Saud's sick sense vengeance. For no doubt the jun would destroy everything Dallan held dear. That's the sort of person he was.

Dallan saw again the broken body of his friend in Weishi House. Driven to suicide. Not much older than Dallan's son.

Guilt surged and tears pricked his eyes. He clenched his jaw to hold in a groan of despair.

He'd honestly thought people would rally to his call for help. More people than two teenage girls. He was a shazi. Maybe Teya was right: people were selfish and untrustworthy. A weight settled on his shoulders and he sagged against the bars of his prison.

'There is no way of doing this with just us, Teya. I'm sorry. I was a shazi to think I could. We'd need an army to go against someone like Han. No-one's going to risk themselves on such a slim chance.'

Teya gave a little gasp. She was staring into middle distance.

Dallan frowned. 'What—'

She shot to her feet and grasped his arm, coughing again. When she could speak, she glared at him. 'What if I could make him *think* we have an army?'

'How will that help?' He slapped the bars and they rang, musical. 'Even if we could get out of this, you can only show illusions to one person.'

Her jaw hardened. 'I lied. I used to be able to fool five, but after learning from Ying, I can do more.'

'How many more?' Hope floated in his chest.

She shrugged one shoulder. 'Not sure, yet. Ten. Twenty, maybe.'

Dallan sighed. 'Not the whole hall full of Juns and House Masters and Mistresses out there, then?'

'No. But I *won't* let Han have my brother.' Her lip curled. 'Don't worry. I don't expect your help to kill Han.' She shook the bronze bars, and inspected where they drove into the sulcrete floor and timber ceiling. They held solid. 'Just help me get out of here.'

Dallan scowled. The weishi had taken his jacket and weapons as well as his boots, which held his lockpicks.

Teya gave a frustrated cry and thumped the bars. She sagged against them with her arms around her stomach and eyes closed. Water puddled at her feet and dripped from her sodden clothes. She must be freezing and there were no blankets here.

He straightened, excitement tingling in his gut. 'I have an idea.' He inspected her soaked tunic and trous. 'Take off your clothes.'

'What?'

He pointed. 'Give me your trous. I think I can get us out of here.' Scanning the other prisoners, he caught the attention of a girl about Teya's age. 'You. Can you keep an eye on the door and let me know if the guards are coming?'

The girl swallowed, and nodded. She hurried to the nearby corner and craned to see through the grill set into the door.

Teya stripped her pants and handed him her dripping trous, glaring. Around them, a muttering and low growling washed through the younger men in the cell. She turned the glare on them.

Dallan did the same. 'Touch her and she'll scream for the weishi. If you want to get home to your families, shut the gouri up. Got it?'

Several men and boys exchanged dubious glances, but they settled.

Conscious of dozens of hungry eyes, Dallan wound the wet trous around two bronze bars at about waist height and began to twist the cloth together in a knot.

Water poured from the bamboo cloth, soaking his bare feet. For a long time, nothing happened. Each turn became more difficult. More water dripped out. Then, slowly, the bronze bars bent toward each other, creaking.

A gasp susurrated around the cell, followed by hopeful whispers. Dallan shushed them and they subsided.

At last, the bars touched and the trous were dry. He unwound and passed them to Teya. She pulled them on and stripped off her tunic, standing bare-breasted and shivering in the cold cell. Blood dribbled down her shoulder.

She half-turned from the crowd and he saw, for the first time, the horrifying burn scars disfiguring her back. Dallan passed her his tunic and she tugged it on with a grateful nod.

He used her tunic to bend the second pair of bars, leaving a gap large enough for an average man to squeeze through sideways.

When it was done, and they were both dressed again, he eyed the crowd. They edged closer, full of hope for the first time. In the other two cells, the occupants pressed against the bars, eyes huge with envy and despair.

A Future, Forged p187

'There's your army,' Teya murmured.

'Closest thing we're likely to get, anyway,' Dallan agreed. He raised his voice slightly. 'There are three cells and only one that has a way out. But I want everyone to get out. Agreed?'

A few exchanged looks and more nodded.

'How?' the girl who'd played lookout asked. 'We have no weapons and no keys.'

'Leave that to Teya and me,' he said. 'We'll get you out. But in return we need help.'

The girl glanced over her shoulder at the other inmates and they exchanged shrugs and nods.

'Right,' Dallan said. 'I need to try one more thing before we leave. We need a distraction. Hang on.' He lowered his outer wards. Hopefully Ying was listening out for him, as she'd promised. He hated to drag the young xintou into this, but he was running out of time and options.

Ying? He waited, his palms slick with sweat and as he anticipated a fight. *Ying?*

Yes! She sounded excited. *I'm here. Is Perrin there? Is Teya alright? The hunli ceremony was all very beautiful. Everything's decorated in Han's colours, though. But Jenna's looking at him like she can't think of anything else. There's a woman in the front row who must be Teya's mother. She looks like her, but dark haired. And her little baby boy is adorable. And I keep having to duck to hide from Mistress Shana. I'm afraid she'll try and Read me or ask me to let my wards down and make me tell her what's going on. But she does seem very focussed on Jenna and Han, so she's probably not thinking about me, is she? I wonder if she—*

Ying! There are four weishi here. We were caught and we're in the cells. Perrin's not here. I need the weishi distracted so we can get out. Can you help?

Oh! Of course. Wait a minute.

There was a sense of absence. Dallan gestured to Teya and squeezed through the gap in the bars. He turned to the girl prisoner.

'Wait here. I'll get the keys.'

'But we could help!'

'I don't want anyone to get hurt.' He shot her the same look he gave his teenage son and she glared in the same, rebellious fashion.

Teya followed him to the cellblock door and they both peeked through the bronze-barred grille inset into the timber.

Where was Ying? The door to the front of house creaked open, letting in light and noise. A small, gold-clad figure skipped down the stairs. The translucent gold veil hid her eyes, but Ying's pouty mouth curved into the most innocent smile he'd ever seen.

Dallan grinned. Beside him, Teya's slim form tensed. He leaned close.

'Wait. Don't waste your strength casting illusions. Wait and see what Ying does, first.'

'I'm fine,' she snapped.

He studied her blue-tinged lips, and the dark stain on her shirt. 'You're not and you need to save your strength for Han.' She hesitated, then nodded.

'Hello!' Ying's cheerful greeting lilted.

Two weishi snapped to attention. The other two rose from the table and hurried over, bowing low. Dallan tested the door. Unlocked. But one weishi faced the cellblock door, so any movement would alert him.

'Oh, dear,' Ying trilled. 'I think I'm very lost. Will someone help me find the bathrooms? Oooh! Is this the prison? I've never seen a prison before. You all must be terribly brave, guarding all these awful people.' She wandered away from the stairs, inspecting a rack of weapons on the wall.

All four weishi turned with her.

CHAPTER TWENTY-EIGHT

DALLAN

Dallan and Teya slipped from the cellblock and behind a supporting wall that protruded into the room. Ying rattled on. It was almost amusing listening to the confused weishi trying to answer the questions tumbling artlessly from her tongue.

Dallan's steel sword and boots lay on a table nearby, along with the boning knife and Teya's bronze dagger. No keys to the cells, though. He edged over, retrieved their things and retreated.

Teya shoved the bronze knife into her belt and watched the weishi while Dallan dragged the boots on and hung his scabbards about his hips. Dallan dug into a pocket in his bootheel and produced a pair of lockpicks.

'C'mon,' he whispered, returning to the cells.

He held out the lockpicks. 'Anyone know how to use these?'

A young man about eighteen or nineteen rose from the floor of the first locked cell, nodding. The rest in his cell stirred, hunger for freedom awakening hope again.

'You need to wait ten minutes after we leave, got it?' Dallan gauged the boy's mettle. He seemed to have the determination needed. 'Then break out everyone here and storm upstairs. The great hall is full of people—and weishi. But if you all work together, most of you will get out. Since you're all being held for ransom, I suspect many of those people could be your families.'

The lad checked with his cellmates. They urged him to take the picks.

Dallan passed them through. 'Make as much noise as you can.'

'Why?' The boy's voice was husky and broken.

'Because you'll be serving as a distraction while my friends and I do our best to kill Jun Fourth Han Gray-Saud. How does that sound?' Dallan grinned fiercely.

The boy lit up and his companions straightened. There were nods and mutterings of agreement. Dallan shushed them.

'Remember,' he said, 'ten minutes. Good luck.'

The youngster held the lockpicks tight against his chest.

Dallan returned to the door, listened long enough to hear Ying still nattering away, and snuck out again. He made his way to the shadowed lee of the wall where Teya waited. She leaned against the stone, sucking shallow, quick breaths.

Ying had seen him pass behind the weishi but hadn't faltered in her chatter. She could talk underwater, that child. He rested against the cool stone for a second while his heart settled.

Then he opened his wards. *Ying?*

Oh, thank goodness! I've run out of things to say!

Sorry. Just warning you. I'm going to have to kill them. I want the prisoners to escape and I need to get the weishi out of their way. Get to the stairs. Try not to watch.

There was a shocked silence, both inside his mind and outside. He forced himself to wait, trying not to swear or push her too hard.

He added, *The prisoners are being held for ransom, remember? They're not criminals, Ying. Most of them are teenagers and children caught out late after curfew.*

Her talk started again, but her laughter sounded forced. One weishi interrupted and respectfully suggested she should be abovestairs with the rest of the guests. She agreed and begged them in honeyed tones if they would help find her entourage as it was *such* a press of people!

Two of them followed her up the stairs. Dallan palmed the boning knife. Not enough room to swing a sword properly and any clang of his steel against their ceramic blades would be loud.

He ghosted from his hiding place. A quick thrust drove the knife into the gap in one weishi's alzin armour, beneath his arm. Into his heart.

The man gargled, clutched at Dallan, and sagged to the floor. Blood spurted from the wound and glistened on his dark uniform.

The second weishi turned. Dallan sliced his throat with the knife. The weishi scrabbled at his neck and slumped against the wall, his eyes wide.

At the top of the stairs, Ying shoved a weishi in the stomach. He overbalanced, arms wheeling. With one hand he latched onto his companion and both tumbled down the stairs in a flurry of arms and legs.

They landed in a tangle at Dallan's feet, swearing at Ying and at each other. Ying remained at the top of the stairs, palms clamped over her mouth, eyes wide.

Dallan plunged the knife into a vein, gritting his teeth against the warm spray of blood and the weishi's gurgling cry. The metallic smell of iron-rich blood filled the room.

The remaining man, wiry and quick, leapt to his feet. He sprinted up the stairs and snatched Ying into his arms. His dagger pricked a bead of blood from her skin. She blurted a faint scream and stiffened.

'Drop the knife or I'll kill her,' he snarled.

Dallan hefted the slim knife, feeling the weight and balance. No good for throwing. Too big a risk of hurting Ying. He dropped it.

'You do realise she's a xintou?' he said.

The weishi sneered. 'A child. And I'm warded. Besides, everyone knows xintou are taught nothing but peace and diplomacy feihua. She won't hurt me. Now—'

He choked, eyes rolling back. Releasing Ying, he clawed at his skull and slumped against the wall, uttering feeble cries. He collapsed and slid bonelessly to the foot of the stairs.

Teya's expression was contemptuous. 'She might not, but I will.'

Dallan used the boning knife and despatched him with a slice to the jugular. More blood seeped across the stone floor, glistening garnet-dark.

Ying hurried down the stairs, avoiding the bloodied bodies strewn across the floor. She threw her arms around Teya's waist.

'You're alright!'

Teya awkwardly patted her. 'I guess. But we have to go.'

'Oh! Of course.' Ying tidied her veil and smoothed her rumpled robe. 'But we can't go that way.' She pointed at the stairs. 'There are hundreds of people and all the important families have weishi. And you...' She wrinkled her nose at Teya's bloodied, wrinkled tunic and wet hair.

'Kitchen's this way.' Dallan jerked his head toward the other entrance. 'And there's a servants' entrance to the upper floors through it. Ying, you should go to Neri. I don't want you involved.'

The young xintou studied the dead guards and swallowed. 'I already am, shenshi. And a xintou's job is to keep the peace in the jundom. Letting slavers take over would *not* be the right thing to do.'

Dallan groaned. 'I can't protect you.'

'I don't need protecting.' Her tone was confident but her eyes darted to the bodies.

He gave up. 'Teya? Ready?'

Her skin was waxen, breathing laboured. She nodded and straightened. 'Let's go.'

CHAPTER TWENTY-NINE

TEYA

Teya crept along in Dallan's wake, trying to ignore the knives stabbing into her chest and the blood trickling along her arm.

Ying held onto Teya's tunic. When Teya hissed at her to let go, the xintou set her mouth and held tighter.

The kitchen staff did little more than gape at the oddly-assorted trio. A few sketched bows to Ying's golden robe without knowing who she was. How could they? Whispers ran around the room until a big, redfaced woman with frizzy hair yelled at her workers to get on with it and stop gawping.

Dallan strode through like he owned the place, bestowing a regal nod on the woman and aiming for a small door in the opposite corner.

Once through, he paused in the cooler darkness of a narrow hallway and whispered, 'I give us five minutes at most before she sends word or checks the prison. We need to move fast.'

The corridor ahead split into three choices. One kept going west, one went north and up a straight staircase. The third was a well-worn, spiral staircase set into the wall.

Dallan pointed to the spiralling risers. 'That's the servants' entrance leading to the Jun First's apartments on the third floor.'

Teya tugged on his sleeve. 'If there are weishi at the top it's a flat-out kill-box, you know that, don't you?'

He nodded, grim. 'But the only other entrance is through the great hall, the main staircase, and the front door of Jenna's rooms. Not an option.'

Teya nodded and smothered a cough. Dallan drew his sword and held the boning knife in his left hand. The staircase spiralled anticlockwise, so he would be at a disadvantage against a right-handed swordsman coming from above, as they would have no wall to interfere with their sword-strikes.

They passed a door on the first floor. Teya struggled for air. Dallan regarded her with concern. She ignored him.

By the time they reached the landing for the third floor, she judged close to five minutes had passed since they left the prison cells. No time to waste. If the prisoners swarmed into the great hall full of guests, chaos would erupt and the shouts and screams would interrupt even the most passionate hunli consummation.

She shuddered at the thought of Han touching the Jun First. Han was almost double Jenna's age. How could the girl admire him that way? How couldn't she see through his charm to the perverted blackness beneath?

'Teya?' Dallan stopped on the stairwell out of sight of the Jun First's door. Drawing her close, he whispered, 'Ready?

She nodded. Her practice with Ying last night had improved her speed in breaking through basic wards, but she still had no way of knowing how she would fare against really strong ones. And the energy that took was huge. She was already weak. What if she couldn't get through Han's? What if she hesitated again? What if—

No. She pushed aside the doubts.

'Ying,' Dallan whispered. 'Once we're in, you make sure the main doors are locked. I don't want his weishi coming in. There are four rooms: the bedroom, a bath room, a bedroom for her body servant, and a sitting room. The sitting room and the maid's room have the doors. But they're at opposite ends of the suite. Lock the sitting room door, first. Got it?'

Ying peered around Teya. 'Yes,' she squeaked.

'Teya,' Dallan asked, 'are you able to hold two different illusions at once on two people again?'

She shrugged. 'Normally, yes. Right now, don't know. I'm not…' his image blurred for a moment '…feeling the best. Probably not for long.'

He swore. 'Right. Then concentrate on Han. I'll keep Jenna out of the way. Do whatever it takes to control him. If I know him, he'll have my dagger in place of his own. Use it, if you can. If not, hold him with an illusion and you can use my sword. I'll have your back.'

She nodded, not trusting herself to speak without coughing. Was he arranging it that way so he could lay the blame on her, afterward? He would be able to say honestly that he hadn't killed Han if she did it for him.

And if she did it—if she gave him what he wanted—he would have no reason to help her find Perrin.

Was she making the right choice? She couldn't think. Her head felt fuzzy. The stairwell was hot and stuffy. She shivered, her arms goosepimpling.

Dallan lay on the stairs, inched upward, paused, then withdrew. He raised two fingers. Two weishi, then.

Teya grabbed Ying's hand and advanced.

Ying whispered, 'Remember—be calm. Open your heart.'

Teya waved her to silence but did draw a long slow breath to try and settle her racing pulse. When she rounded the last corner, the two weishi straightened.

'Who—'

She inserted an image of two gold-glad xintou women into their thoughts and demanded entrance. Bowing, the weishi shuffled aside without question.

'That's so scary,' Ying whispered.

'Shut up,' Teya replied. 'I'm concentrating.' Cold sleeted across her skin and she struggled to lift heavy feet to the next riser.

Dallan appeared beside her and leapt past on silent feet. She rendered him invisible. He thrust his knife into the nearest weishi's inner thigh, cutting the leg's main artery. Then he smothered the man's cries and eased him to the ground until he stopped struggling.

Teya focussed on the second, blanking Dallan and the wounded weishi from his mind. He stood, unmoved and unmoving, while Dallan scored the knife across his throat.
p200

Blood pooled, forming thin, scarlet waterfalls over the steps.

Ying whimpered and scurried aside, lifting her robe hem. 'You didn't have to kill them!'

'Hush!' Teya snapped.

Dallan wiped his blade on a fallen weishi's black and copper uniform. 'They were Han's men, Ying. Not Jenna's. Anyone allowed this close to Han is complicit in his plans.'

Ying's eyes were huge, but she nodded.

Teya felt nothing. She was past compassion for anyone close to Han. She'd seen the lengths Han's weishi would go to for him. They deserved no mercy and no guilt.

Squaring her shoulders, she prepared the next illusion. And the steel hammer that would smash Han's wards. This time she would not hesitate. This time she would be ready for him.

This time she would set Perrin free and get the diyu out.

Dallan thrust the door open.

'Ah! There you are.' A voice broke the bedroom's silence. 'I was wondering when you'd arrive.'

Teya froze, burning inside. That smooth, sarcastic tone was unmistakable.

CHAPTER THIRTY

TEYA

Han rose from a chair by the fireplace and tied a dark blue house robe tight around his lean frame. On the huge, silver-curtained bed, Jenna lay, still clothed in her black-and-silver wedding gown, her eyes staring blankly at the canopy above.

Teya's knees weakened. Had he murdered her, already?

Dallan swore and hauled out his steel sword, setting himself before Teya and Ying.

'Wait.' Teya growled. 'I can do this.'

Gritting her teeth, she formed the hammer and struck at Han's wards. But her blow was weak; his wards strong. They held firm. Hatred raged black in her blood. She could gouri-well do this! He deserved to die.

Han held out his hand toward the second armchair, which faced the fire.

Teya tensed and struck his wards again. A tiny crack appeared. Hot triumph washed through her body, lending false strength. One more would do it.

This time it would work. She would be free of him forever.

'Teya!' A small, blond boy leapt from the armchair and limped across the room.

Teya gasped, her concentration broken. Perrin hurled himself at her and she dropped to her knees with her arms wide. She gathered his slim body to her and held him close, trembling, savouring his warmth. His arms twined around her and he buried his face in the curve of her neck.

'I thought you were dead,' he sobbed. 'I thought I'd never see you again. I was in prison, then the cells with lots of people and it was awful and stinky and you didn't come for me.' He sniffled and wiped at his nose. 'Why didn't you come for me?'

Guilt gnawed at her, leaving a gaping hole in her chest. 'I tried. I was hurt and then I couldn't get into the prison.' She stroked hair from his face. 'But I'm here now.'

'Then,' Perrin said, smiling, 'this nice man came and got me out of the cells and guess who he gave me to, Tey. You'll never guess. It was our mam. He found our mam for us. Isn't that great? An we gotta baby brother. He's little, but we can be a family again, like I always wanted.'

She heaved herself upright, swaying. Perrin wrapped his arms around her hips.

Teya looked at Han.

With a whimper, she clutched Perrin closer. Four weishi held Dallan prisoner, swords at his collar. Gen-kin held Ying at dagger-point.

Yet another weishi rested a sword tip on the Jun First's breast. She didn't react. Her eyelids closed and reopened, but she didn't seem to see where she was.

'Teya?' Perrin tugged at her tunic.

She didn't reply, just stared at Han, who smiled coolly and said, 'So, girl, what's next?'

'Can we stay, Teya?' Perrin begged.

She held Perrin close. Her heart swelled and closed her throat. She couldn't lose him again. Not now.

'You said you'd let us go if Dallan was killed,' she said. 'You have him now. Let us go.'

\#

DALLAN

Dallan sighed. He couldn't blame her. This was a no-win situation. There were too many strong-minded people here and she was unwell. She swayed on her feet and her skin was waxen. No way could she break through Han's wards and hold strong illusions for him and six weishi at once.

He opened his mouth to reassure her, but two blades pricked against his collarbones. Han sent him an amused look and Dallan held his tongue, helpless. He'd been a zift.

Three times he'd underestimated Han and this time would get them all killed. Oh, Han would gloat a little. It was his way. But the steel in his gaze said he had no intention of letting Dallan live.

A sick sense of inevitability settled like cold mud in his gut. And Shana—wherever she was—couldn't possibly let Ying go free, either. So his stupid, childish belief that enough people, working together, could do good would cause the death of two young women with their whole lives ahead of them.

And Perrin? Dallan examined the boy who was Teya's heart and saw why she was so desperate to save him. The lad looked at his sister with such open, worshipful adoration and uncomplicated love that Dallan's chest ached. She had suffered so much. Lost so much. To have one person who cared for her unconditionally and to lose him would break her.

Was there a way to convince Han to let her and Perrin go? If so, he couldn't think of the words. Nor would Han care to hear them from him.

Bitter regret brought bile to his throat. If he'd been less harsh all those years ago in Weishi House… if he hadn't rejected Han so contemptuously, with the judgemental arrogance of youth… perhaps they wouldn't have come to this.

Ying wailed Teya's name and tried to yank free of Genkin's meaty grasp.

Teya's attention flickered to the young xintou. 'Let her go, too? We'll all leave. Quietly. You'll never see us again, I promise.'

Han's mouth pulled sideways into scorn. 'You can't be that naïve, child. I can't let her go. And your freedom was conditional on *you* killing Dallan. But you were too soft, weren't you? Or did his all-for-one-and-one-for-all romantic ravings about helping the masses get to you?'

He chuckled. 'He's always been an idealist. Now you know his cause is hopeless. The people he's been trying to rally—the ones with power and wealth—are also the ones with the most to lose if I don't control the jundom. Introducing unpaid labour helps them.

'Tell you what.' He tilted his head. 'I'll give you a second chance.'

He moved to a low table near his chair. On it lay a collection of small blades: a kpinga, a karambit, several daggers. He lifted one. Light slipped sleekly along the steel blade and Dallan tensed.

The weishi around Dallan hadn't bothered disarming him. After all, there were four of them. His sword still hung at his side. And Han now brandished the matching dagger, dangling it like a lure, tempting him to attack. Dallan held himself in check.

Han held it out to Teya. 'Take this and run him through, girl. Then I'll let you and your brother go free. But I'll have witnesses to the fact you murdered a first-family member in cold blood. So if you ever break your word and speak out against me, you'll both die.'

'I don't believe you,' Teya said, but hope and doubt warred on her face.

Dallan held in a groan.

Han shrugged. 'I know you don't, but think about it. I don't need either of you. Never did. You're both useless to me.'

Teya blanched so pale Dallan thought she might faint. But her eyes narrowed, assessing Han. What was she thinking?

Perrin clutched at his sister's leg. 'Teya?' His voice was shrill. 'What's going on? I don't understand.'

A Future, Forged p207

She crouched and pulled him into a hug. 'It's alright, Perrin.' She kissed his forehead. 'It'll be alright.' Her voice cracked.

'Don't!' Ying shouted. 'Don't do it, Teya. You're not like that. You can't.'

Gen-kin held the young xintou firm.

Han laughed. 'Of course she is. She knows very well that everyone is out for themselves. She's smart. She'll do what she must to survive.'

He held the knife out. 'Won't she?'

CHAPTER THIRTY-ONE

TEYA

Teya put Perrin aside and told him to stay against the wall, in the corner. She sucked a breath, holding in a cough. Then she closed the gap between her and Han, her skin crawling at the thought of being so close to him.

But there was no other way. He was right. She would do what it took to survive and to protect Perrin. Especially if Han believed them both to be useless. That made getting Perrin away even more important.

And herself.

If he knew she was xintou, he'd never let her free.

She accepted the blade, hefting it. The handle was still warm from his touch, and a little too big for her hand. The steel gleamed, lethal.

On unsteady legs, she walked over to Dallan. The four weishi parted, letting her close without taking their blades from his body.

She swallowed and squared her shoulders. 'I'm sorry. Truly.'

His shoulders slumped. 'I understand. You have to do what's right for you and the boy.' A warped smile etched his eyes in sadness. 'Maybe I was naïve to think I could get people to do what was best for the whole jundom. Coming from my privileged background, I forgot how desperate people in your situation are. And how greedy are the ones who already have enough.'

Teya tightened her hold on the dagger, her arm shaking. She looked away from his honest empathy and fixed on his chest. All she had to do was stick this blade into him and she and Perrin were free. They could go anywhere. Get out of this city. Go to Jadid, maybe, and start again.

Get away from the slavery coming to Mamalakah.

But would Jadid be far enough?

Dallan gently covered her hand where it cradled the knife. The weishi around him tensed.

'It's alright, Teya,' he said. His gaze flicked to Han. 'I know you're not well, but you *can* do it. Remember what Ying said and be calm. Be open. Trust.'

It took a moment for the message in his words to filter through the drubbing of blood in her ears. Teya stilled. He wasn't accepting his fate so she could survive. He was asking her to use her gift. To try and cast illusions into the minds of seven people, one of them strongly-warded.

She should have known. No-one was that altruistic.

If she tried, and failed Han would kill her and keep Perrin as a slave.

If she killed Dallan she would be free.

But that would condemn thousands of children like Perrin to slavery.

Surely they could leave, too? She couldn't be responsible for the whole jundom. It wasn't fair.

'Teya?' Perrin's querulous voice made her look around. His confused adoration slowly segued into fear. 'What are you doing to him?'

Gouri. She switched back to Dallan and clenched her teeth. She would get one shot at this.

Behind Han, a door opened in a wall painted with landscapes both beautiful and exotic with blue skies and green trees. The door closed again and Mistress Shana strode over and stood beside Han, smiling condescendingly at Teya.

'Well,' she said, folding her fingers across her stomach, 'so you've come home have you, girl?' She pointed at Dallan. 'And brought your father a gift, I see. Good girl! Go on, then. Kill him.'

Teya choked, the knife falling to clank on the timber floor.

#

DALLAN

Dallan's lungs stopped working. Father? Of course she was Han's daughter. He was a fool to have missed it. The auburn hair, the strong jawline. He'd assumed Teya's father was Helva's first hunlin.

Gouri! Kin-child or not, that made *Teya* Han's true Jun-Heir, not Helva Connor's toddler. What the diyu was going on? Why had Han hidden her away?

Then the worst of the situation dawned on him. Shana was here. No way could Teya break through the wards of a trained xintou and insert an illusion without being felt. And that would give away what Teya was.

Right now, Han and Shana didn't know the girl was xintou. If they found out… If Teya revealed what she could do and failed to kill Han, then the jun would never let her go. He would keep her and hold Perrin as hostage. Use her xintou gifts to further his own ambitions. To control his followers. Why have one xintou when you could have two?

Dallan wanted to howl in frustration but controlled himself. He should never have brought her here. He had to find a way of shielding her. Had to try. For Teya's sake. He might not be able to save the jundom, but perhaps he could save her and Perrin and Ying.

'Enough games, Han,' he said. 'What do you want?'

'Why, nothing but your death, my dear old friend.' Han collected a wine bottle. He poured a glass of the light purple liquid and held it to the glow of the electric bulbs overhead. 'I have everything else, now. The Jun First's throne is in my control. I have an heir for the Jun Fourth title.'

His scrutiny travelled over Teya and Perrin and his lip curled. 'A *male* heir who is whole in body and mind this time.' He sipped his wine, some secret glee lifting the corners of his mouth.

Whole in body and mind? Dallan studied young Perrin. Was the boy's intelligence or stability in question? He seemed bright enough.

p212

Han gestured with the half-full wine glass. 'And now I have a young hunlinna who adores me and will do everything I ask without question.'

His eyes gleamed. 'And I mean...everything. And anything. It's quite refreshing how eager to please she is. Though I daresay I'll tire of it. But by that time the slavery laws will be enacted and I can have my pick of nubile young things.' His grin widened. 'Won't that be nice?'

Near the servants' door, Teya made an inarticulate noise and retreated toward Perrin.

Dallan inspected Jenna's inert form on the bed. The young Jun First's chest lifted and fell. A faint, dreamy smile curved her lips.

'What have you done to Jenna?'

'Me?' Han pointed to himself. 'Nothing at all. Well, nothing she didn't enjoy.'

Dallan reigned in the urge to lunge at the man and said through gritted teeth, 'You know what I mean. Have you drugged her?'

Mistress Shana's deep-throated laugh shook her shoulders and breasts. 'You weishi-trained types are far too straightforward in your thinking.'

She threw a sneer at Jenna. 'The girl is happy. Look at her. She was miserable before. Unsure of herself. Afraid to rule. She needed us. The jundom needed us.'

Across the room, Ying shoved her veil onto her forehead. 'You...you're *controlling* her! How could you do that?' Her fists clenched at her sides. 'You're a Bonded Xintou. You're supposed to stand for everything that's good for the jundom. What's true and honorable. I didn't believe Teya when she told me what horrible things you'd done. But you *have* turned against the House, haven't you?'

Shana snorted. 'Don't be silly, girl. Xintou are the House Mistress's puppets. She says jump and we're supposed to mindlessly jump? Mistress Rua is old and out of touch with what the jundom needs. The House needs new blood. Mamlakah needs new blood. The Zah-Hill family has become weak-minded. Without Han, the jundom would be crushed by debt and absorbed into Melcor within ten years. I *am* doing what's good for the jundom. You're too young to understand.'

Ying said nothing, but her lips were thin, her eyes blazing.

'Enough, Shana,' Han said. 'You'll get your chance to convert her to our cause, later.' He gestured to his weishi, who collected Dallan's dagger from the floor and tossed it to the jun.

Han pointed the dagger at Teya. 'Come, girl. Finish the job and you can go free. Kill him. My word is good. Remember? I promised your mother a good life. She has it.'

Teya's head snapped up. 'You gave my mother no *choice.*'

'Of course I did. She had the choice of coming to live in my house in luxury and producing my heir, or continuing to live in poverty after I burned her house to the ground.'

'With us in it! You told Gen-kin to burn us alive because we weren't good enough to be your heirs. A girl and a cripple.'

Sickened, Dallan could only groan. That explained so much. Han had always been a stickler for perfection in his lovers. He hated deformity of any kind and thought women inferior. Of course he wouldn't want a girl, or a boy with a twisted leg, as heir. But to burn them alive in their own house...

Han heaved an exaggerated sigh. 'Enough histrionics, girl. Decide.' He held out the dagger. 'Kill Dallan and go free, or don't and die. I don't care, either way.'

Enough. Dallan gathered his strength. He might not be able to save the whole jundom; he might not have an entire army at his disposal, but he could jiche-well save the life of three children here and now.

And, if he was any judge of Teya's character at all, his actions might not be in vain. Perhaps he didn't need a whole army.

Perhaps he needed a few, key people who were willing to help at the right time.

But how to convince her?

CHAPTER THIRTY-TWO

DALLAN

Dallan studied Teya. The conflict there. The indecision. She was driven by a deep desire to protect her brother. The one person who loved her. The one person she trusted… ahhhh.

Understanding relaxed his shoulders. Now he knew what to do.

'Afraid to face me, yourself, Han?' Dallan forced his words to emerge light and scornful. 'Afraid I'll beat you this time?'

Han laughed and Shana joined in. The jun flipped the dagger over twice, catching it neatly.

'Yes, I seem to remember you tried once before, back at Weishi House.' He tapped the blade on his chin. 'Something about me being an unscrupulous hundan, wasn't it? I beat you then and let you live because I still cared about you.' He held the dagger out. 'Very well. Care to try again?'

Dallan hesitated. What choice did he have? He caught Ying's stricken gaze, lowered his wards for a moment and allowed her access to images too complex for words, then added,

Make sure she understands?

She nodded, tears coursing down her cheeks.

He raised his chin, confronting Han. 'Will you let Teya and Perrin go if you win?'

Han shrugged one shoulder. 'I have no need for them.'

'Then let's do this,' Dallan said. Han flipped the steel dagger expertly to him. Dallan caught it.

#

TEYA

Teya gaped as Dallan's weishi guards lowered their weapons and let him approach their master. Why was he doing this? He had no hope of defeating Han. He said he'd never beaten the jun and Han had trained at Weishi House longer. And even if he seemed close to winning, the weishi would kill him. Why would he offer to fight Han? It made no sense. What did he have to gain?

One of the weishi guarding Dallan strolled over and pushed her and Perrin into a corner of the vast room, giving the two men space. Gen-kin, Han's shangwei, jerked his head and swapped places with the weishi. Now a lesser man guarded Ying. Gen-kin grinned at Teya and blew her a kiss.

'When this is over, sweetheart, you and I are going to have some fun.'

Teya said nothing but cold prickled across her skin.

His sword point lay at her collarbone, but his attention lay on the two men circling each other.

Dallan unsheathed his sword and hefted his returned dagger in his left hand. A knife-edge grin played on his lips. Teya waited, heart in her throat. Perrin complained she was holding him too tight. He wriggled free and sat in the corner, scowling.

Teya couldn't stop watching Dallan, trying to understand.

Dallan struck. Han deflected the blade with a *tang* of steel on ceramic and spun aside. Dallan danced closer. Sliced at Han's leg but again his blade missed. The jun laughed. Dallan's steel arced at his neck.

He would be beheaded.

Teya held her breath. But Han shifted at the last second and his blade slickered across Dallan's ribs.

Stumbling out of reach, Dallan touched his chest and checked the bloodied smear on his fingertips. Teya bit her lip. It must be just a scratch? Han had barely touched him.

Dallan swore and raised his sword again. Teya sputtered a sigh. He was alright.

Dallan deflected a lightning-fast strike and scored blood across Han's arm. The jun inspected the cut and nodded.

'First blood to each of us, then. Well done.'

'I've been practicing, too.'

A sense of being observed itched at Teya. Ying's eyes were fixed on her. The young xintou lifted her little finger. It took Teya a moment to remember that was the signal between xintou who wished to speak telepathically. She lowered her outer wards, keeping watch on Dallan and Han.

He's doing this for you, you know. Ying's tart thought dropped into Teya's mind.

What?

A ghost of a sigh. The sense of impatience. *He told me. Just before the fighting. He didn't want you to have to kill him. And he doesn't want Han to know you're a xintou because then Han would hold you prisoner. He said to make sure you and Perrin get free if he falls.*

Teya stilled, unable to wrap her mind around the thought.

Did he tell you to say that? Teya demanded.

No! Ying's reply was indignant. *He told me to get you out of here and to make sure you understand that Han can't know you're a xintou.*

Her attention fixed on Shana with something akin to hatred. *But I'm willing to try and stop them if you are. That woman should* not *be Xintou. I want her taken before the Law Mistresses. I don't care if they* do *throw me out of the House for telling tales about my betters. She's not better. She's horrible.*

Why would he do anything for me? He hardly knows me, Teya demanded. Something hot and painful burned in her chest.

There was a pause, then Ying replied, her mental voice sounding surprised. *Because he cares about you, Teya. He's a good man. He's trying to do the right thing.*

He cared?

Dallan leapt back from a thrust that would have carved his chest in two. His sword beat Han's aside. His dagger tip sliced a red line across Han's cheek.

Han bared his teeth, feral. Dallan chuckled.

Teya recognised the feeling in her chest: hope. Hope and also the impending awareness of hopeless loss to come. Because Dallan was risking everything.

No. He was *sacrificing* everything to give her a chance at freedom. He had a family. A life of luxury. He was in no danger of being made a slave. But he had tried to rally the whole jundom to a worthy cause.

And failed because she had let him down, time and again. But he was still willing to possibly sacrifice his own life to protect her?

The pain faded and a kind of gentle warmth spread from her chest into her limbs. Her lungs relaxed and the urge to cough faded.

Ying's voice sounded again. This time with a hint of desperation. *What are you going to do, Teya? I'll help if I can. I might be able to distract Shana for a little while, but she's stronger telepathically than I am. And whatever she's doing to control Jenna is an ability I've never heard of. I'm scared. If Dallan dies, then Shana will control me, too. Dallan's doing this so we'll* all *have a chance. But it's up to you, now.*

Teya closed her eyes.

Yes. It was up to her. But she couldn't do it alone. She would need to trust Ying; rely on her and Dallan, both.

And that scared the diyu out of her.

A Future, Forged p221

CHAPTER THIRTY-THREE

TEYA

Ying, Teya said, *I can't hold illusions for this many people at once. I'm too sick.*

She recognised the fever symptoms now. Her skin burned even though she couldn't stop shivering, and she was having trouble concentrating. Her right arm felt thick and hot. The tunic sleeve was stained all the way to her wrist.

Oh! Ying's thought returned. *Then keep on Jun Gray-Saud. Stay calm and have faith. You have to let your anger go. Then you'll be strong enough. You can do it.*

Teya said nothing for a moment, trying to release a tremor of fear.

Teya? What do you want me to do?

We have to divide them. Do what I say, when I say. First we deal with the one holding you and then Gen-kin—the one holding me. When he lets me go—

I'll distract Shana!

No! She's too strong for you. Wake up Jenna. We need a witness. Get her out from Shana's control. That will distract Shana enough. I can work on the others. We have to hope Dallan can keep Han occupied and stay alive.

But—

Just do it, Ying.

Teya raised her wards.

Dallan let out a cry and staggered away from Han. The tip of the jun's ceramic sword was red and Dallan pressed a palm to his hip. When he moved into the fight again, it was more slowly and he limped. Teya's chest ached with captive warning cries. He wouldn't last much longer.

Han twirled his sword, smiling lazily.

'Not enough practice, eh Dal,' he said. 'And I don't have a lot of time for playing so we'd best finish this soon.' He sketched an ironic half-bow. 'I do, after all, have a very large jundom to run, now.'

Teya swallowed a jolt of fear and concentrated on the weishi holding Ying. He had weak wards and it took nothing to shatter them. She inserted a sound illusion. The weishi's attention turned to the outer door, leaving Ying unobserved.

Next, Gen-kin. She put aside her hatred for the man who had lit the fire on Han's orders and tried to follow Ying's advice. The hammer shimmered into view. She strengthened the illusion she had for him. Then she smashed his wards into dust.

'Hey, Gen-kin,' she said. He grunted, keeping his attention on Dallan and Han.

'Remember when you lit the fire and tried to burn me and my baby brother alive in our house?'

His gaze snapped to her and he sneered. 'Yeah. How did you get out, anyway? My men sealed that place tight.'

She bared her teeth in mock-sweetness and stripped away the layer of false memories she'd laid in his mind five years before. She exposed the recollection of what he'd done, but changed the memory of why he'd done it. And who had been in the house.

'You let us out,' she murmured. 'I'm sorry your hunlinna didn't make it, though. You were so angry about her death. I can't believe you're still working for Han, after what he did.'

The shangwei's jaw dropped. With one thick hand he patted his sweat-shining forehead.

'I…I remember. Han said my hunlinna had betrayed us. I couldn't believe it. But he said he had proof. He…he locked her in with you and made me set the place on fire. I heard her screaming. He left. I let you out and tried to get to her.'

He rubbed at his temple. 'But…' his brows snapped together '…how could I forget something like that? Oh, gouri! The screams!' He put a palm over his ear.

Teya put on her best innocent front. 'Shana can control what people think. Maybe…' She bit her lip. 'I shouldn't have said anything. But I wanted to thank you for setting us free.'

He waited, panting and staring blankly at her. She replayed the fake memories of his hunlinna screaming. His body jerked. Then she added a hazy one of Shana telling him to forget.

Colour fled his cheeks, leaving him so grey she thought he might vomit.

Instead, he directed a flat, hard scowl on Mistress Shana. He stalked to where she stood behind the bed, observing the duel between Han and Dallan with every appearance of smug delight.

Teya sagged against the wall, her knees weak. She smothered a cough.

'Perrin!' she hissed. He limped to her side and clung to her, darting frightened looks at the fighting men. 'See those two weishi?' She pointed at the two men standing flatfooted, watching Dallan and Han. 'We need them out of the room. Can you sneak out that door and do the same thing you did when we stole from that rich lady the day we got caught?'

'Fall over and yell loud and pretend I'm hurt?' he whispered.

She nodded. 'When they come out to see what's happening, tell them a bunch of people are attacking everyone downstairs.' She hadn't heard any screams, but they were three floors up and she hadn't been listening.

'Are they?'

'I gouri-well hope so. Go.' She wrapped him in a swift hug and he scuttled around the wall, unnoticed.

In the room's centre, Dallan's foot caught in a rug as he retreated. He collapsed and rolled over one shoulder, rising to his feet not far from where she stood. Han advanced, the light of victory blazing in him. Dallan gulped for air. Blood stained his shirt in three places, his trous in two.

'Han!' Gen-kin's hoarse shout stopped the jun. Han edged off to one side, keeping Dallan in view.

'What?' he snapped. 'I'm busy.'

'You gouri hundan!' Gen-kin growled. 'You made me murder my own hunlinna then you got this unveiled jiaoji-whore to wipe my memories!'

He dug his bronze dagger further into Shana's throat and held the xintou before him like a shield. She seemed quite calm, just a slight frown creasing her forehead.

Ying's face distorted into feral anger as she concentrated, her attention on Shana.

'What the gouri are you talking about?' Han demanded. He lowered his sword a fraction and scowled at his shangwei.

A shrill scream erupted outside in the sitting room. Perrin.

Teya readied herself.

A Future, Forged p227

p228

CHAPTER THIRTY-FOUR

TEYA

The two weishi hurried out in the direction of Perrin's scream. Teya threw her next illusion at the weishi guarding Ying. He should hear the sounds of dozens of people yelling in the distance. The crash of swords and more screams.

He glanced uncertainly at Han, who ignored him. He left Ying and went out into the sitting room.

Teya nodded at Ying. The young xintou scowled at Jenna, lying motionless on the bed.

Shana blinked, shook herself, and struggled in Gen-kin's grasp. He pricked the dagger into the skin of her neck and she stilled.

Han was arguing with Gen-kin, now, glowering. Trying to convince Gen-kin his hunlinna had died of a wasting illness, not in a burning house. Teya re-inforced the memories of her death in the fire and Gen-kin roared a denial.

Teya risked touching Dallan on the shoulder. He whirled, staggered, and straightened. His skin was sheened with sweat and blood, his chest heaving.

She pointed at Han. 'Together?'

Dallan wouldn't betray her. She knew that now. The question was, would she have the strength? Could she control her feelings? The well of hatred she felt for Han bored deep into her heart.

A lightning grin flashed across Dallan's bloodied lips. 'Together.'

Too many things happened at once.

Shana yelled for the weishi and glared at Ying. The tall woman tried to push Gen-kin's arm aside, contemptuous.

The shangwei dragged his knife across her jugular. She gargled, clutched at the gaping, spurting wound and fell across the corner of the bed.

Jenna awoke and sat up, shrieking.

Han screamed and clutched at his skull as the bond to his xintou was ripped from his mind.

Teya bared her teeth in triumph.

Gen-kin launched himself at Han, his face twisted into mania. Dallan ran at the jun from behind.

Teya steadied herself on the wall as her knees buckled and the room bled into sepia tones. She gasped for air that seemed to hold no sustenance.

She had to keep herself together, just a little longer.

Two weishi burst into the room, one hauling a limp and bloodied Perrin by the collar.

Teya stilled.

One of them inspected Jenna, then Shana, then Ying's triumphant expression. He smacked the pommel of his dagger into Ying's temple. She crumpled into a heap of gold silk.

Teya took a half-step in her direction and stopped. She had to *think* not just jump in.

Han fended off Gen-kin and Dallan, both, with sneering ease.

She had to help Dallan. This was their last chance.

She centered on Han's wards and drove her hammer against them again and again. But her concentration faltered as rage swelled at the sight of his arrogance.

She wasn't strong enough. Panic strangled thought. Acid and heat boiled in her stomach. She had to kill him. Had to stop him.

Han fought off Gen-kin's wild attacks and Dallan's weakened ones, but they were slowly forcing him into a corner.

The two weishi leapt to their jun's aid.

Dallan deflected a blow from one but staggered.

Teya forced emotion aside and hit out again at Han's wards. A crack appeared. Hope blossomed. She struck again. The crack widened.

Han snatched a kpinga throwing knife from the table and hurled it. One blade sank deep into Dallan's left arm.

Dallan cried out, hoarse and agonised. Han stepped close, a sneer curling his lip. Dallan's arm came up to block.

Too late.

Han drove his dagger into Dallan's chest.

'No!' Teya's scream scraped her throat raw and broke her concentration. She ran to Dallan's side. He fell against her, blood pouring from the wound.

A Future, Forged p231

Too much. Too much.

She pressed a hand to his side. Hot blood gushed between her fingers, slick and scarlet. Smelling of iron. He slumped to his knees.

'I'm sorry,' he whispered. 'I'm sorry.'

Then he toppled sideways and lay still, his eyes staring, blank. His last breath gurgled free on a sigh and a spray of blood.

'No,' she choked. 'Please, no.' Ice congealed her limbs, her lungs, her muscles. He couldn't be dead. He couldn't.

She looked at Han, still living. Still fighting Gen-kin. Likely to win, now.

White-hot anger exploded; consumed her, mind and body.

Perrin lay unmoving in one corner, his hair matted with blood. Ying was so limp she must be dead.

Yet Han fought on. His expression was grim, but he had Gen-kin on the back foot now, driving him across the room.

Teya yanked Dallan's steel dagger from his lax hand and rose. She put every hope of vengeance, memory of agony, moment of pain and hatred into her mental hammer and smashed at Han's wards.

But the image melted away and vanished like water. Her gift deserted her. His wards remained unbroken.

She stopped, lost. She couldn't do it. He was too strong.

Han slashed his blade across Gen-kin's arm and the weishi roared.

No. The memory of Ying's stern instructions floated into Teya's thoughts. She closed her eyes.

p232

Hatred wouldn't help this time.

She slowed her breathing. Her mother's loving face danced before her. Dallan's amused, wry smile. Perrin's delighted laugh. Ying's wide-eyed faith.

Trusting. Opening her heart and mind. Believing that Dallan and Ying were right. As she should have done, before. That was the key.

The hammer appeared in her thoughts; shining steel. Red-hot.

Now she could be what Dallan and Ying had seen in her all along. And she could save her mother and baby brother. Perhaps even Perrin. Perhaps even the people of the jundom.

Calm and certain, she smashed the hammer, over and over, against Han's wards. Fine cracks appeared. Hairline fractures in the smoothness protecting Han's mind.

He drove his sword through Gen-kin's chest, pulled it free and wiped it clean. Then he turned to Teya.

Smiling, she crushed the last of his wards, leaving ash and the memory of protection. Then she obliterated his inner wards.

Only when his whole, sordid mind lay exposed did she fill it with the illusion she had prepared.

Then she moved over to the window, and waited.

He screamed. Screamed and threw his weapons aside. Screamed again and batted at his body, crying for someone to put it out. Dropping to the ground, he rolled on the bloodied rug.

But nothing would put out the flames.

A Future, Forged p233

The remaining weishi stopped and gaped at him. Han continued to scream until blood frothed at his lips and bloodvessels burst in his eyes, turning them red.

Only then did Teya douse the flames and add one last touch. Now he saw Dallan, alive and well, standing before him.

Mocking. Laughing.

Han staggered to his feet and grabbed at the illusion, but it danced out of reach.

Step by step she lured him closer. When he stood before her, she removed Dallan and let Han see her.

He sucked a shuddering breath and checked his hands, stroking the smooth skin there. Then he raised his gaze to hers.

'What the…You! Where's Dallan?' He glanced around.

She jammed the Johnston dagger hilt-deep into his heart. He twisted away, mouth agape, the dagger still protruding between his ribs.

'You gouri, little—' Blood dribbled from between his lips.

She pushed at his chest.

The glass window exploded outward. He plummeted three stories to the courtyard below.

More people rushed into the room as Teya's legs gave way and she folded to the floor.

Jun Neri's horrified expression was the last thing she saw.

p234

CHAPTER THIRTY-FIVE

TEYA

A room swam into view. A familiar room. Dim-lit but with a hint of daylight creeping around the edges of thick curtains. Jun Neri's guest bedroom.

Teya lay in the over-soft bed, too weak to do more than drift in and out of memories and dreams. Someone came and tried to feed her. She turned away. She didn't deserve their consideration.

Dallan had died because she hadn't believed he really wanted to help; hadn't been willing to work with him—until it was too late.

Perrin. Ying. All of them. Dead because of her stubbornness. Why was she even still here? Why hadn't she died, too?

Everyone she cared about was gone.

And she had cared. She hadn't wanted to admit it. Hadn't wanted to let them close in case they proved to be as self-centred as everyone else. But they hadn't betrayed her. She had failed all of them. And the jundom.

Han might be dead, but without Dallan to lead the fight against slavery, someone else would step into Han's shoes. That was how the world worked. She knew that too well.

She tossed, unable to get comfortable. Unable to sleep or wake properly. Strange dreams haunted her sleep and memories haunted her awakening.

Someone called her name, over and over, tearful. Two voices. Then a third. Achingly familiar.

She opened eyes sticky with sand and sleep.

A woman's face swam into view. Tired, sad, but joyful at the same time.

'Mother?' Teya whispered. 'Mother?'

Helva Connor folded Teya into her arms and cried into her shoulder. 'It's me. Oh, Teya, yes.'

Rocked in her mother's soft arms, Teya finally released the tears she had been holding in for five years. She wept until she was too weak to hold onto her mother and had to slump onto the pillows. Helva made her drink something tartly sweet that soothed her raw throat.

'Sleep now,' she whispered, kissing Teya's forehead. 'It will be alright. I promise.'

Teya tried to keep her eyes open but they were too heavy. She managed to ask a question, though the words came out slurred. 'Perrin and Ying?'

Helva kissed her cheek again. 'They're both alive, sweetheart. They're fine. We're all fine. Thanks to you. Sleep now.'

'I need to see him! Perrin,' she managed.

A few seconds later, Perrin's wiry body snuggled next to her in the bed. He said her name, sniffled, and curled himself close.

Her heart a little easier, Teya slept.

#

'Do you really have to go?' Tears shimmered on Ying's lashes.

Teya touched the long bundle in her lap and nodded. 'Dallan wanted to give his sword and dagger to his son.' Her fingers tightened on his steel blade, wrapped in his cloak. 'Neri said the dagger disappeared when Han's body was taken into the Chinshi. She thought Jenna took it.' She thrust aside the memory of his death. She would deal with that, later. 'So the least I can do is return the sword and let Dallan's family know how he died.'

Ying sighed and gripped her ankle. The huoche driver clucked to the four che-ma hauling the trundling vehicle and pulled on the reins when they stamped and huffed with impatience.

Seeing Ying's genuine worry, Teya clambered down and hugged the younger girl. Ying's smile wobbled into place. She wore again the yellow house robes of an apprentice xintou and she had recovered her sunny optimism, but every once in awhile she cried for no reason and Teya didn't know how to help her.

'I'll miss you.' Ying sniffed. 'And Perrin. Everyone's leaving!'

Teya laughed. 'And you're going back to Madina. Besides…' she scanned across Asalam's uneven skyline and shuddered '…it's time to move on. Now that Mistress Rua has heard the testimony of all the juns and xintou that Shana and Han either controlled or blackmailed into helping, there's no way the slavery laws will be brought in. Dallan's family need to know that, too. They need to know he didn't sacrifice himself for nothing.'

A lump clogged her throat and she had to scrub at her eyes.

'But,' Ying said, 'you're supposed to be jun to the Gray-Saud line, now. I know you don't want to, but Dallan once told me that the best rulers are the ones who don't want the job.'

Teya shook her head. 'That's what someone who's never had to do a job they hate says. I'd be a terrible jun. I'm too restless and impatient.'

'You'd be wonderful!' Ying insisted. 'You're smart and you'd champion the people in the Migongs. *Make* the other juns look after people.'

Curling a lip, Teya kept her reply as gentle as she could. 'We both know what would happen if the other juns found out I was xintou. Even with my limited powers. They'd be terrified of me.'

'Then it should be Perrin or little Zhan,' Ying said.

Teya pushed her words away. No-one born of Helva Connor could be allowed a jun title. Han Gray-Saud and his Xintou, Shana, had chosen Helva because of her latent xintou genes. Combined with Gray-Saud's own latent genes, they had intended to breed their own pet male xintou to use as a weapon. Shana had examined Perrin at birth, and he wouldn't be a xintou.

Her new little brother, though… Han must have kept him for a reason. Only time would tell.

She gazed toward the Chinshi and shuddered. 'No. Giving the Gray-Saud title to that cousin of Han's was the best way. He seems like a good enough person.'

Ying's shoulders slumped. 'But you'll be all on your own! Your mother and Perrin are going all the way to the other side of the jundom. How will you get to them?'

Teya shrugged one shoulder. Her right was still stiff and weak after days of infection and lack of use. The Healer House woman who'd tended her had expressed surprise she'd survived at all and told her she would lose some use of the arm.

'Teya?'

'Sorry.' She smiled at Ying. 'Neri gave me enough money to get Dallan's sword home and then get to Gaton, where my mother is headed. She has family there—on the Wen-Gates estate. I'll see what it's like before I decide to stay. Maybe…' she lifted her face to the peridot sky and sucked in the smell of freedom '…maybe I'll see where my feet take me.'

'I wish you'd come to Xintou House with me. I can't believe Mistress Rua is letting you leave! She's always going on about how dangerous untrained xintou are.'

'I think she realised I'd be a bad influence on all of you. Look what happened to you!'

Ying threw her arms around Teya and hugged her. 'I'll never regret meeting you,' she said. 'You made me realise how important it is to stand up for what's right, even when you're scared and even when it might ruin your life.'

'No. Dallan taught us both, that. And a lot more.' Teya sighed. 'And you taught me how to let go of my anger at Gray-Saud. I owe it to both of you to find out what I'm good at. To make something of my life. And someone has to keep an eye on things to make sure the slavery people don't get out of control again. I owe him that, too.'

'Will you come and visit me in Madina?' Ying begged.

'I will, I promise.'

Ying eyed her with suspicion.

Teya chuckled. 'That's another thing I learned from Dallan: always keep your promises.' She climbed onto the cart then extracted her purse from her pocket and withdrew her mother's tiny gold locket.

She pressed it into Ying's hands. 'To remember me by.'

Ying smiled and held it tight in her fist.

Teya nodded to the driver. The che-ma whickered and pulled her toward a new life.

She looked back twice. Ying was still watching.

Teya waved, knowing she would never again be alone, and turned north.

THE END

If you enjoyed A Future, Forged, please go to your place of purchase and leave a review. It helps.

Other books by Aiki Flinthart

Discover other titles by Aiki Flinthart
at: **www.aikiflinthart.com**
Including:

The Blackbirds Novels (Historical Fantasy)
Blackbirds Sing (#1)

The Ruadhan Sidhe Novels (YA Urban Fantasy)
Shadows Wake (#1)
Shadows Bane (#2)
Shadows Fate (#3)

The Kalima Chronicles (YA Adventure/Fantasy)
IRON (#1)
FIRE (#2)
STEEL (#3)

The 80AD series (YA Adventure/Fantasy)
80AD Book 1: *The Jewel of Asgard*
80AD Book 2: *The Hammer of Thor*

80AD Book 3: *The Tekhen of Anuket*
80AD Book 4: *The Sudarshana*
80AD Book 5: *The Yu Dragon*

Sold! (Contemporary Romance/Adventure)

Short Story Anthologies
The Zookeeper's Tales of Interstellar Oddities
Return
Elemental
Connect with me on Facebook
Twitter: @aikiflinthart
Instagram: Aikiflinthart

APPENDIX

Story facts and background

Kalima means 'World' in Arabic. The planet was settled by idealists from Earth seeking a world without conflict. The planet's sun is a K-type orange star in the Gliese 167 system. Rayleigh scattering of light combined with atmospheric dust high in copper oxide, gives Kalima a pale teal-green sky.

The sun's orange colour led to dark blue and black-leafed plantlife. Kalima is third planet from this sun. Gliese 167 is a cooler sun than Sol, but Kalima is closer to their sun than Earth is to Sol. Kalima's. 14 month year and its axial tilt and elliptical orbit means the southern hemisphere (the location of the colony cities) has a long spring-summer-autumn cycle and a short, 2-month winter. The northern hemisphere has larger extremes of weather and is, as yet, uninhabited.

Kalima has an active geologic past, which formed continents, volcanoes, oceans and rivers. But, until the terraforming teams arrived, Kalima was bare of life. The rocks created by the presence of life on Earth—such as marble, oils, methane, coal, chalk, limestone, or banded ironstone—do not exist on Kalima. The few iron deposits in existence are iron-sand beaches created by volcanic activity, and meteoric iron. The planet has high levels of copper and a vast desert of copper-rich soil on one of the other continents has contributed to the levels of copper oxide dust in the atmosphere, which causes the green sky.

A Future, Forged p243

The colonists chose a lifeless planet and paid to have it Terraformed and seeded with life and complex ecological webs. Initial terraform teams were sent to Kalima on faster-than-light ships, while colonists took slower, jumplight sleep-ships to allow the teams sufficient time to complete the infrastructure. Five hundred years after departing Earth, the first of three ships arrived, carrying twenty thousand carefully selected colonists.

Mainly of Chinese, Arabic and European descent, colonists were chosen and screened for their desire to live a peaceful, agrarian existence. Kalima's twenty-one Jun families descend from the original twenty-one Funding families who financed the expedition.

Two hundred years after settlement, supply ships from old Earth ceased and colonists were obliged to be self-sufficient. Lack of iron prevented the colonists from creating a high-tech society, forcing them to live in semi-medieval conditions, although many old ideas and skills have been retained.

Electricity generation through wind or water power exists in limited form. The ability to make telescopes, lenses and microscopes has not been lost and, although medical understanding of surgery, physiology and healing exists, it is limited by the lack of modern technology. Many books on old technologies have been preserved and, some colonists retained information regarding warfare and weaponry—the basis of knowledge in the Weishi House.

Kalima society is substantially feudal, the Jundom of Mamlakah being ruled by 21 Juns, under the leadership of the

Jun First and two Jun Seconds. Melcor, to the north, and Jadid, to the south, are also feudal societies but Melcor's society and economy is built on slavery. Shemal is a democracy.

Languages are mixed. A version of English, borrowing many words from Arabic and Mandrin, is the dominant language in Mamlakah, the first colony site. Similarly, cultural crossovers are normal. Women and men wear robes or high-collared shirts and trous (loose trousers tied at the waist). Robes are worn indoors or while employed in non-active trades and management positions. Otherwise it is common for trous and shirts with jackets or cloaks to be worn.

Women wear their hair long and loose or, if of a higher caste, long and up in elaborate hairstyles. Men in Mamlakah wear their hair long and tied back in a mawei (low ponytail or plait). Women wear a transparent veil that covers the eyes and nose only. The veil is symbolic of mystery and high ranking rather than an indication of women's inferiority.

In Mamlakahn society, women are, basically, equal in standing to men. They may be Juns or Trade Masters in any House and are free to undertake any training and job. In any colony, however, women are more valuable than men. Built into the psyche of the colony is the need to protect women that has continued into today's thinking.

Weishi House came into being primarily as protection for women of childbearing age from natural hazards, though its scope expanded as the colony grew. Women are the bearers of the next generation and the survival of a colony depends on how quickly women can give birth and outstrip death rates.

A Future, Forged p245

The need for high birth rates, and genetic diversity, led to the practice of kin-children. In the early days of the colony, a couple unable to have children was a wasted pairing. Women needed to have children by several fathers in order to keep the gene-pool as diverse as possible.

People/Places/Things

Adeghal – capital of Shemal

Ahmar – Red (Ahmar Mountains run down the Eastern boundary of the kingdom)

Alzin – an aluminium-zinc alloy.

Asalam – northerly seat of the Zah-Hill family.

Aswad – Black (Aswad ranges run down the centre of the kingdom)

Ceramic Swords are made of zirconium dioxide

Chengdu- capital of Melcor

Days are: Ahad (one), Ithnan (two), Thalatha (three), Arba'a (four), Khamsa (five), Sitta (six)

Ghadeb – 'angry' (Ghadeb sea to the northeast)

Gharb – west (Gharb ranges run down the Western boundary of the jundom)

Gunpowder = saltpetre + sulphur + charcoal

Jiali – 'home' – Capital city of the Ma-Safra family lands

Jadid (New) Jundom – south.

Kabir – big (the Kabir river runs through the middle of the kingdom and empties into Melcor's port 700 gongli away to the east)

Kalima – World. Earth-sized planet. Kalima has a 6-day week and a 5-week month. 30 days per month. 14 months in a year and 422 days in a year – two days at the end of the year are not part of any month and are called yirun and er'run. Axial tilt and slightly elliptical orbit means northern hemisphere has extreme seasons but southern is mild with short winters and long growing seasons.

Kuaisu River – 'fast/rapid' river (wraps around the eastern side of Shanzhai)

Luna-Yi – red moon

Luna-Er – blue-white moon

Madina – capital city of Mamlakah. Palace - The Alkazar.

Magnal – magnesium aluminium alloy – light and strong

Melcor – second kingdom to be settled – to the northeast of Madina and on the Ghadeb sea. Reached by trade on the Kabir river.

Metsa – the river running through the western section of the Ma-Safra Jundom, near Newmec. It eventually joins with the Kabir just north of Madina

Mianshou – end of year 2 day celebration during Yirun & Er-run.

Plants are dark blue-black-leafed (absorbing different, greater range of spectra and reflecting less green)

Seryeh River – 'quick' river (wraps around the western side of Shanzhai). The two rivers join and become the Kabir, just north of Madina

Shanzhai – seat of Jun Second Koh-Lin.

Sulcrete – concrete where the binding agent is sulphur rather than lime (limestone does not exist on a planet without an organic geologic history)

Yan – 'flame' = yanstones

Yirun & Er'run – extra two days at the end of the year. Mianshou = End of year celebrations last for these two days and anything done on these days (apart from violence) is unpunishable.

Zalam – slums within Madina

…..

Trade Houses

Artist House (purple veil/purple hat)

Healer House (white veil/hat, grey robe)

Jiaoji (Courtesan) House (red veil)

Merchant House (green veil/green hat)

Messenger House (orange)

Miner House (grey hat)

Trades House (brown hat/veil)

Weishi House (black veil/black hat)

Xintou House (gold veil, gold robe) Mistress Rua

…..

Jun Families

Jun First Jenna Zah-Hill – Silver and Black.

Jun Second Carval Ma-Safra - silver and purple.

Jun Second Alric Koh-Lin - silver and green.

Jun Third Han-Asad - gold and black (Vassal to Zah-Hill)

Jun Third Yu-Smith - gold and green (vassal to Koh-Lin)

Jun Third Lee-Hay - gold and purple (vassal to Ma-Safra)

Jun Fourth Wen-Gates - copper and purple. (vassal to Ma-Safra)

Jun Fourth Han Gray-Saud - copper and black (vassal to Zah-Hill)

Jun Fourth Neri Qin-Turner - copper and grey (vassal to Zah-Hill)

Jun Fourth Knight-Hun - copper and green (vassal to Koh-Lin)

Jun Fifth Jaber-Lun - red and purple (vassal to Ma-Safra)

Jun Fifth Seif-Li - red and green (vassal to Koh-Lin)

Jun Fifth Zhou-Issa - red and teal (vassal to Koh-Lin)

Jun Fifth Easton-Green - red and black (vassal to Zah-Hill)

Jun Fifth Amoudi-Mann - red and grey (vassal to Zah-Hill)

Jun Sixth Ortega-Miller - blue and black (Zah-Hill)

Jun Sixth Quing-Mai - blue and grey (Zah-Hill)

Jun Sixth Price-Khan - blue and green (Koh-Lin)

Jun Sixth Yasif-Do - blue and teal (Koh-Lin)

Jun Sixth Khoury-Ban - blue and purple (Ma-Safra)

Jun Sixth Blake-Swift - blue and indigo (Ma-Safra)

Johnston house - blue & green tartan

…..

Mandrin

Numbers and distances and times

Yi – one (Luna-Yi = first moon – reddish)

Er – two (Luna-Er = second moon – silver)

San - three

Si - four

wu - five

Liu - six

Qi - seven

Ba - eight

…..

Chi – approx 33.33cm

Zhang – approx 3.33m

Gongli – kilometre

…..

Months:

Yiyue – first month of the lunar year (1st month of spring)

Eryue – second (spring 2)

Sanyue – 3rd (spring 3)

Siyue – 4th (summer 1)

Wuyue – 5th (summer 2)

Liuyue – 6th (summer 3

Qiyue – 7th (summer 4)

Bayue – 8th (summer 5)

Jiuyue – 9th (summer 6)

Shiyue – 10th (autumn)

Shiyiyue – 11th (autumn)

Shi'eryue – 12th (autumn)

Shisanyue – 13th (winter1)

Shisiyue – 14th (winter2)

…..

Words:

ading – antiseptic/disinfectant

Bai - to pay respect / worship / visit / salute

Bei – flower bud

Bi – coin

Che-ma – cart horse

Chuizi – a hammer-strike

Erheyi – two-in-one

Feihua – nonsense, rubbish.

Gangzhi – made of steel

Gongren - worker

Gu – archaic - legendary venomous insect / to poison / to bewitch / to drive to insanity / to harm by witchcraft / intestinal parasite

Hepan – river plains

hunli - wedding

Huoche – wagon/truck/van

Jiali - Home (name of Ma-Safra city)

Nari – double-edged sword

Jiaoji – courtesan

Jin - gold

Jinbi – gold coin

jiu – rice wine/liquor/alcohol

Jun - monarch/lord/gentleman/ruler

Junren – soldier/serviceman/military personnel

Khaan – king/horde leader (Mongolian)

Kuaisu – fast/rapid

Kuai long – fast dragon

Kui - Chief/head/outstanding/stalwart/exceptional

Lanhua - orchid

Lanse – blue (lancha tea)

Lu – deer

Luotuo – camel

Manxing – slow poison

Mawei – ponytail

mayao – anaesthetic

Mianshou - - to avoid suffering / to prevent (sth bad) / to protect against (damage) / immunity (from prosecution) / freedom (from pain, damage etc) / exempt from punishment

Molian – to temper oneself/ to steel oneself/ self-discipline/ endurance

Nai – mother

Quan - dog

Rong – salamander

Runiu – dairy cattle

Shangwei – captain (military rank)

Shanzhai – fortified hill village/mountain stronghold

Shen – deity/soul/spirit/mysterious

Shenshi – my lord

Shi - is / are / am / yes / to be

Shifu – teacher

Shunu – my lady

Si-xing – death penalty / to act recklessly

Song – sponge (cake)

Tiebi – iron coin

Tongbi – copper coin

Watu – poison frog toxin

Weishi - guardian/defender

xiao – similar to/resembling (ie: xiao-cat)

xiang - elephant

Xintou – thoughts/heart/mind

Xiongshou – assassin

Xituo – to cleanse/to purge/ to wash away

Xue – blood

xun – herb

ya-zheng - correct (literary) / upright / (hon.) Please point out my shortcomings. / I await your esteemed corrections.

Yan – flame

Yinbi – silver coin

Yinghan – man of steel/tough guy, unyielding

Yongbing – mercenary/hired gun

Zaohua – good luck/nature (the mother of all things)

Zhi – to stop/prohibit

Zitan – red sandalwood

Zuoce – left side

…..

Insults/swearing

diyu – hell/underworld

Feihua – nonsense / rubbish / superfluous words / You don't say! / No kidding!

gaisi – damn it!

gouri - lit. fucked or spawned by a dog / contemptible / lousy, fucking

hundan – scoundrel/bastard/hoodlum/wretch

huo-zui – living hell/suffering/hardship

jian-gui – curse it/to hell with it

Jiba – penis (vulgar)

Jiche – pain in the ass/damn!/crap!

Jijin – elite/best of the best

qusi – go to hell/drop dead

salai – make a scene/raise hell

shazi – idiot/fool

suilie – disintegrate/shatter into pieces

Wasai – exclamation to express amazement/wow!

zhen-shide - Really! (interj. of annoyance or frustration)

. . . . .

Rabic

. . . . .

Days: Ahad (one), Ithnan (two), Thalatha (three), Arba'a (four), Khamsa (five), Sitta (six)

Ahmar – Red (Ahmar Mountains run down the Eastern boundary of the kingdom)

Al Mamlakah – the kingdom

Alcazar – from Al-qasr – fort, castle, palace

alem'erekh – fight

Aswad – Black (Aswad ranges run down the centre of the kingdom)

Badiya – desert

Dafdae - frog

Gharb – west (Gharb ranges run down the Western boundary of the jundom)

Herq – burn

Heryeq – fire

Hilya – trinket/ ornament/jewel/finery

Iblis - Devil

Istilqa – sleep

Jabal – Mountain

Jadid – New (name for the southern jundom)

Jiyl – generation.

Kabir – big (the Kabir river runs through the middle of the kingdom and empties into Melcor's port 700 gongli away to the northeast)

Kalima – World

Khiba – tent

Madina – City

Malik – King

Mamlakah – the kingdom

Menzel - home

Mhareb – warrior/fighter

Mumit – deadly

Nasir – vulture (nasiri = plural)

Sabat – coma, lethargy, torpor

Sahalia - lizard

Shaytan – demon, fiend, serpent

Selb – Steel, betterment, loin, crucifixion

sery'eh – Quick (Seryeh River to northwest of Shanzhai)

Tabib – doctor

Zalam – Darkness

Zanbur – hornet, wasp

Zibal - scavenger

Zinzana – cell/prison

…..
p256

Insults/swearing

Hamagi (hamag = plural) – uncivilised, barbaric

Haraami – thief

Hmar – jackass

Jahim - hell

Kaddaab – liar

Kalb – dog

Kalet – filthy street bastard

Khara – shit! (frustration)

Saafil – base;loathsome

Waa faqri – damn!

Wisix – dirty/filthy (morally)

Zift – Idiot